THE WELSH BOYS

Chris Boult

About the Author

Chris studied in Nottingham in the late 1970s. He joined the OTC and the TA and later served as a short-service officer in the regular army before joining the probation service in 1986. He served as a probation officer in various settings and at different levels, working mostly with high risk offenders and often closely with both the police and the prison service. He retired from service in 2015. He started writing novels in 2013, and this is his sixth book.

Website: chrisboultauthor.co.uk

Previous titles:

In the Shadow of the Bayonet

Out of the Shadow

Recovery

Green Terror

Identity

Acknowledgements:

Thanks to all involved in this process. A particular thanks to: my wife and my sister for help in proof reading, my publisher, Dave Bott and Titanic Brewery for their assistance. Also thanks to Sheila King of Chapters bookshop in Stafford for her support for local authors and to all other suppliers of the books. Thanks to Martin Nolan and Dave Clough for their advice on Emma's business activities.

To: my mother for her influence and guidance from the Welsh side of the family.

'Avoiding danger is no safer in the long run than exposure. The cautious are caught as often as the brave.'

Helen Keller – American writer

Author's note:

The book is set in mid-Staffordshire and North Wales. Emma and Rory's story takes place in the present between the spring of 2016 and June 2017. Events in North Wales, however, start in the spring of 1986. Many of the places are real, although again I have indulged in some poetic licence, with other places being entirely fictional. All the characters are also fictional.

The history of the Howell brothers from Porthmadog develops from the nineteen eighties and is an attempt to portray many of the themes that feature in the lives of offenders, their families and the agencies that deal with them.

Glossary of terms:

In consecutive order:

Breach – the mechanism in the probation service to return offenders to court or to prison for non-compliance.

DIY – Do It Yourself.

GPS – Global Positioning System a satellite-based aid to mountain navigation.

Niasmith's rule – A formula for calculating time based on distance and ascent for mountain walkers developed by William Niasmith, a Scottish mountaineer in 1892.

Prison security classifications – Category A-D from the highest to lowest level of security.

Police rank structure – DCI – Detective Chief Inspector.

D of E – Duke of Edinburgh Award Scheme for young people.

VPU – Vulnerable Prisoner Unit where prisoners are held for protection from other prisoners.

The Punishment Block – where those prisoners subject to breach of prison discipline can be held, now more often called the Care and Support Unit.

CPS – Crown Prosecution Service.

MAPPA – Multi Agency Public Protection Arrangements.

PPU – Public Protection Unit.

Tariff – The minimum time a life sentence prisoner must remain in custody before any consideration of release.

HR – Human Resources; the team in any organisation that deals with personnel.

Chapter One

Spring 1986.

Pregnant at sixteen, Bronwen Howell stood at the bus stop, waiting. Cold, isolated, frightened. She wondered where she would go and how she would manage, but she knew that after her father had thrown her out of the house the previous night that there was no prospect of return. She was alone.

She looked back towards Porthmadog and cried. She didn't really want to leave, but felt that she had no choice. She thought of the nights at the local youth club. Was it worth it, those tumbles in the dark? He said he knew what he was doing and that she'd be alright, but obviously he didn't.

The bus arrived. She climbed aboard and asked for a single to the end of the line. Where would it take her? She wasn't sure, but anywhere far away would do. As she sat alone, troubled, anxious and uncertain, she fell asleep.

'Time to get off, love,' the bus driver announced as the bus came to a halt.

She looked up and gathered her things. She stumbled off the bus, unsure of exactly where she was, but she recognised a landmark and knew that she would be safe.

***

It was spring 2016. Rory let Bracken run free off his lead. 'Come on, Bracken,' he called, eager to complete his walk in time to get back to work. Their lovely wedding and the honeymoon had all gone so well and so quickly. The venue in Coppermere was great; an old country manor-house that offered a venue for the civil ceremony, reception, evening entertainment and accommodation all on one site. They had been fortunate and were able to respond at relatively short notice when they were offered a cancellation. Otherwise, the waiting list was frustratingly substantial.

The wedding was the culmination of their commitment to each other in a relationship forged in unusual circumstances. Having grown up together as brother and sister, the eventual discovery that they were not blood relatives had offered them the opportunity for their love to bloom. They knew each other well and were well suited. Family and friends had been able to come together for a true celebration of love.

Emma still owned her flat in Birmingham while they decided how they would make arrangements work in their new life together. In many ways, it made sense to keep the flat as a base for her travels, or they could rent it and use the income. In the meantime, however, Emma had effectively moved in with him into a ground floor self-contained flat within the shared house in Millfield. The flat was a much better option than the room he had previously in the same house. Rory liked the house, the people and the location, but he felt it was only fair to offer to make a fresh start. They needed to get out of renting and into the property market in any event, but that would be the next stage, and there was a deposit to save first.

Emma had already left in the early morning to return to her busy life. She was heading to the airport for a flight to Frankfurt for a business meeting.

Travel would dominate her day and she anticipated returning late. Rory would have dinner ready. Bracken ran through the fields as ever, excited with anticipation at what he might find. He returned with a stout stick and invited Rory to throw it for him. As the stick hit the water, Bracken launched himself into the canal without hesitation. Ducks quickly took to the air and cattle looked on from the far bank. Bracken duly returned with stick at the ready, eager for another chase.

What will await me on my return to work? Rory wondered. He had tried not to think about it while he was away, but as a keen young probation officer that was hard. How would his cases fare without him? How many people would have fallen foul of the regulations and been returned to custody? There was no point in guessing, he would know soon enough. It felt like a whirlwind from events prior to the wedding and the excitement that was generated, but he knew that he was content. Emma was the right choice for him and she had assured him that she felt the same.

Returning to work after leave had become more difficult, even for Rory, in light of so many recent changes to the service. Old certainties had vanished as new mantras emerged. Government had seen fit to separate the probation service some time ago into a privatised low- and medium-risk element based on different private contracts and a national state-maintained public high-risk service. Transition, implementation and early performance were all generally regarded within the service as something of a muddle and a mess. The model was clearly politically driven and not primarily based any empirical evidence of effectiveness. Whether or not individuals believed that private sector involvement could improve efficiency and outcomes, there was little doubt that the political imperative for it to be seen to work would override any indications to the contrary. For both arms of the service this was a considerable culture change. Roles expanded, staffing reduced and support services were centralised.

The question for officers like Rory, however, remained as to whether the public were better protected and whether the chances of rehabilitating offenders improved under the new arrangements or not. At best you had to be sceptical, he concluded. It was certainly a less comfortable environment in which to work, with more pressure and less discretion. Ironically, though, some of the more onerous political restrictions placed on the service before these changes did begin to ease in time. Specifically, for example, the return of greater professional discretion on whether or not to instigate breach against those subject to supervision for non-compliance, necessitating either a return to court or to custody, or to allow supervision to continue. Excessive use of breach had undoubtedly artificially inflated the prison population and put extra pressure on a service already struggling to cope with the number of inmates.

Rory still liked his job but did begin to wonder whether he would still be doing it in ten, fifteen or twenty years' time. Old assumptions about the security of a job for life had long since gone.

Having returned Bracken to the flat, Rory set off from the shared house in Millfield to his office base in Upper Lowbridge, trying to start his day with a positive frame of mind. Greetings and congratulations were quickly dispensed with, and almost forgotten, as he returned to his desk and switched on his computer. The usual torrent of emails awaited him with reference to developments on some of his cases, requests for information and allocation of further work. He set about ordering and prioritising the list, quickly deleting the messages of little value. As expected, breach action had been taken on several cases in his absence, some a disappointment, some expected and others inevitable. In the mass of information, one message stood out relating to one of his cases: Karl Pritchard.

Karl had a history of mental illness, exacerbated by illegal drug use and fuelled by shoplifting, theft and deception. He was due back in court facing fresh charges and a report had been requested prior to sentencing. He was on remand at HMP Dovegate near Uttoxeter. Rory quickly arranged a visit.

***

Emma landed in Frankfurt after a hurried journey from home. *Life back in the fast lane*, she thought to herself as she reflected on recent events. Emma was amused by how

4

long it had taken Rory to realise that they were destined for each other. His eventual proposal came as no surprise to her. The wedding had been wonderful. Well attended and a real celebration of love, ambition and optimism for the future. Maybe for her too there was a sense of contentment in contrast to her prior experience of hectic, unfulfilling and transient relationships.

Back to business, but not as usual, she felt different. Her world had been materialistic but now it had been exposed as hollow and pretentious. Love was more appealing. Stability and security seemed desirable and attainable – a welcome prospect and not a straight-jacket.

Her day unfolded with few surprises; contacts were renewed, new business opportunities were identified, new projects were initiated. Life would return to being busy. Emma liked to be busy, to be stretched, and she therefore liked the dynamism of business life. She also relished the chance to combat sexism at every opportunity and forge a way for women to be successful in business on their own merits.

She had experienced her share of rejection, put-downs, inappropriate comments and unwanted advances, but she had learned to deal with men and to confront their expectations where necessary. For the most part, this had been a successful strategy, but she found the continued encounter of old-style inappropriate attitudes to be disappointing.

Emma had felt that she had gained her natural affinity with business from her father. Business had always been part of the family conversation and ethos. She was initially attracted to the freedom of the market and the opportunity to progress and make money. She found that she had an eye for an opportunity and the leadership and social skills to take others with her whilst promoting a product. Success had come fairly easily and quickly, but now she had a growing sense that it was time to move on.

Chapter Two

Bron had recognised a street corner as she got off the bus, a street corner that evoked happy childhood memories, memories of sanctuary, warmth and care. She knew that a few houses down from the corner shop, the cafe and the barbers would be her aunt Megan's house. Not a real aunt, but a family friend and her favourite adult she could remember from her troubled past.

She stood and knocked the door in anticipation rather than dread.

'Aunty Megan, I'm in trouble,' she said in tears as the door opened.

'You'd better come in then, child,' was the kindly response.

There was a long pause.

'What kind of trouble, child? Do you want to tell me about it?'

'No.'

'Alright then,' Aunt Megan said calmly, without judgement or condemnation.

Bron remembered first visiting the house back in the 1970s and now in the mid-1980s she observed that it hadn't changed much. She just remembered how kind Aunt Megan had been and felt safe for the first time for as long as she could recall. It was one of her social workers who had put her in touch with Aunt Megan, she thought. Yes, Bron remembered visiting sometimes with her mother, but often alone. She always liked it there and feared going back home. Leaving Aunt Megan was always so hard she remembered.

'A nice cup of tea I think for you then, Bronwen. Two sugars, isn't it?'

Bron just smiled and felt instantly secure.

'Now then, what's on your young mind?' her aunt asked, fearing a range of possibilities, but none of which would surprise her. Bron's family were well known in the area. Her father was a bully and her mother struggled to cope to do the basics; to put food on the table, keep the children clean and safe. She struggled as her own mother had struggled and many like her. Unemployment, poor health and housing had all taken their toll on the Porthmadog community over the generations. Bron was perched on the end of the couch, her aunt sat opposite. She had placed a slice of homemade cake in front of her and smiled.

Bron ate it quickly and slurped her tea without embarrassment.

'Well?' asked her aunt again.

Still with tears in her eyes, Bron leaned forward.

'I'm pregnant, Aunt Megan.'

'Oh, I see. How long?'

'Just started.'

'Have you seen a doctor yet, child?'

'No.'

Through the tears, Bron began to tell her aunt about how her father had reacted when she let it slip that her period was late. How he had ranted and shouted at her, how he had thrown things round the room and how her mother had just cowed down in a corner by the window. Aunt Megan listened with distain and disappointment, but not surprise, knowing that was exactly how she would have expected Bron's father to have behaved; how his father had behaved and probably his father's father.

Bron continued.

'In the middle of his rage, he simply pointed to the door and my mother nodded meekly. I ran upstairs, grabbed a few things and left the house without even a goodbye.'

'You poor child. You're safe now.'

'Can I stay with you, Aunt Megan?'

'Of course you can, Bron. You're here now.'

***

After a few days, Aunt Megan felt confident in raising the difficult issue of Bron's pregnancy and her future plans. The opportunity arose as they were sitting down with a cup of tea, with Bron seeming relatively relaxed.

'You do realise, of course, Bron, that you do have choices regarding this pregnancy?'

'You mean you want me to get rid of the baby?' Bron responded angrily.

'No, no, child. It's for you to decide. I just wanted to make sure you were aware of the options and had thought about it. That's all, dear.'

'What do you mean?' Bron responded, having calmed down a little.

'Well, obviously you could keep the child. Yes, abortion is an option, but there is also adoption. Have you thought of that?'

'What? Give my baby away?' Bron shouted, becoming tearful. 'No,' she shouted emphatically. 'This is my baby and nobody is going to take it away from me. This is something special just for me, it's mine!' she cried.

'Alright,' said Aunt Megan calmly 'But you do realise what a responsibility it can be to be a parent, and what hard work it can be?'

'How can it be hard work when you love a child? Anyway, I'll get help, won't I? I'll be able to get a flat. I'd really like that.'

As the conversation continued, Aunt Megan was left feeling concerned. It was clear to her and unsurprising that Bron's understanding of what was to come was very limited and naive. She accepted it for what it was, however, and didn't feel that it was her role to try to persuade Bron to do anything other than to take the path that she had already chosen. She wouldn't mention it again. It was done. Bronwen would have the child, for better or for worse, she concluded.

Rory drew into the car park at HMP Dovegate. He passed through the routine security checks without incident and proceeded to the visits hall, where he waited for Karl to arrive. It wasn't too long before he recognised the sad-looking figure of Karl Pritchard leaving his escort behind and approaching Rory at his allocated table. They shook hands and Rory quickly got down to business.

'So how are you, Karl? What's been happening?' he asked.

'I'm sorry, Mr Scott, I have let you down again…'

'It's not me you've let down, Karl.'

'Well, it feels like it is. See, you have been good to me and I've fucked up again. I stopped taking the medication and things soon spiralled out of control. I went from cannabis to alcohol and back to heroin so quickly I couldn't keep up the payments and started shoplifting again. The shops soon recognised me and warned me off, but I ignored them. Then, of course, I got caught, by which time I'd also done a couple of street robberies and the police nailed me for that too. I'll go down this time, won't I, Mr Scott? About five years, probably…'

Rory started to unpick the story in more detail, recognising that Karl's prediction was about right – five years for robbery, given his history. His only potential saviour was his mental health condition, but he didn't feel optimistic that the court would allow Karl psychiatric treatment rather than imprisonment. Karl's response to treatment had not been good in the past and some assessments had suggested personality disorder rather than illness, which made the prognosis for successful treatment remote. Custody seemed inevitable. Damage limitation was likely to be their most realistic approach. Rory knew he would do his best but could not excuse street robbery, whatever the context.

Rory gathered what other information he required to complete his report and left the prison. He wondered how useful an experience prison could prove to be for Karl. The public would be protected in the short term, of course, but if Karl lacked the capacity to learn or to change, the longer term prognosis was poor. Rory knew that prison could be a brutal place for the likes of Karl. He would be likely to succumb to offers to supply him with drugs, get into debt and face intimidation to pay. His family would not support him so Karl would likely struggle through his sentence, asking for transfers between prisons to escape the bullies and spending time in Vulnerable Prisoner Units and in segregation. Rory hoped things might work out better but knew that they probably wouldn't.

He set off for home, to walk Bracken and prepare dinner. The prospect of sharing the events of the day with Emma was something to look forward to. He had managed the initial adjustment back to work, but unsurprisingly, the experience had left him with mixed feelings. He drove on, trying to put such thoughts behind him as he approached home.

Chapter Three

As expected, when Karl Pritchard came to court, he was sentenced to imprisonment. The Judge listened carefully to the arguments in mitigation, particularly in respect of Karl's mental health. However, as he rightly argued, transfer from prison to hospital was always possible within a sentence if necessary and, as Karl's mental health had stabilised on remand, there was no justification for a hospital order. He was sentenced to four and a half years imprisonment.

Rory would wait to see where the prison authorities placed him. He anticipated work to monitor Karl's mental health, programmes to address his thinking and offending, particularly in relation to the robbery offences, and planning for his release on licence. Placing Karl following release was not going to be easy, given his history. Rory would need to consider that in good time. Supportive housing at the least, or some form of therapeutic community, seemed the most likely to be effective but places were hard to obtain. *A challenge to come*, he thought. They parted on good terms and Rory hoped that he had at least helped to offer some realism, hope and optimism to this vulnerable young man.

***

Emma was already starting to consider their future beyond the shared house. She had visions of a cottage in the country and was even talking of giving up work and raising a family; quite a shift for a career girl, so Rory thought! He was not sure that he was ready for children yet and just wanted to enjoy time together for the immediate future. A house move, they both agreed, however, was a realistic prospect.

They talked about it over dinner. Somewhere mid-way between her Birmingham base and Rory's office seemed realistic. They consulted the map and identified several areas to explore. They planned to visit villages out towards Shropshire or south of the county, nearer Wolverhampton, such as Perton or Brewood. Financially, they were in a good position to put down a deposit on their first house and envisaged being able to sustain a reasonable size mortgage. They felt lucky in that respect but acknowledged that they had both worked hard to be in this position.

Rory felt settled in the team at Upper Lowbridge but could move to a different team, or one of the prisons further south; both Featherstone and Swinfen Hall had their appeal. Featherstone dealt with medium secure category C adult male prisoners and Swinfen Hall the full range of risk categories for young offenders. Emma was less settled at work. Marriage had been an opportunity to review things for her and she felt that maybe it was time to strike out on her own and start a new business, independent of the bigger corporate world. At this stage, however, she was unsure of the form such an idea could take. It would require more thought and research.

The following day at work, Rory met a police officer he knew on his way back from court. He remembered dealing with him in regard to a sex offender case. He'd moved, Rory remembered. They recognised each other instantly.

'Oh Hello. Jason, isn't it?' asked Rory.

'Yes, Rory, you're a probation officer, right?'

'Yes, I think you were on the move when we last met.'

'Yes, I'm a sergeant now in the fraud investigation branch, a big change from dealing with sex offenders!' Jason remarked.

'How's that going?'

'Interesting, but fraud is such a big problem now and we simply don't have the resources to deal with it effectively. From small to big time crooks, most just get away with it because we don't investigate them. Even when we do, cases are often so complicated that the prosecution rate is very low. Trials can collapse and juries can be left so confused after months of difficult evidence that they really don't feel equipped to make a decision, in which case they seem to acquit and all that effort is wasted.'

'Unless they actually were innocent, of course?' countered Rory.

'Rory, believe me, there are so many filters before investigation and throughout the process that, by the time we get to court, we know they are up to their neck in it, but we still have to prove it to the satisfaction of the jury and that's very difficult.'

'Frustrating then?'

'Absolutely, I'm even beginning to miss the sex offenders, Rory!'

'Oh well, I wish you luck. I'm dealing with a fraudster at the moment. Sarah Bridges, serving five years for her part in a bogus holiday sales scam.'

'Oh, Sarah, she was my first case in the branch. Give her my regards!'

Rory returned to the office after having to cover court duty at short notice. Sarah was actually a case he needed to give some attention to. She was due for release fairly soon and he needed to make some preparations. Like many fraudsters, she had a house to return to, so accommodation at least wasn't a problem. The offence was internet-based and so returning to her home area was unlikely to cause any serious community reaction. In fact, she had been careful not to defraud local people and was well thought of in the community and active in many charitable good causes. Actually, he remembered there had been quite an outcry at the time, but not from the community feeling aggrieved. Instead, it had been surprise and even indignation that such a local 'worthy' had been so accused. People simply couldn't or didn't want to believe it, but Sarah was a callous fraudster underneath her facade and had quite knowingly conned ordinary people out of large sums of money.

She offered apparently attractive, 'exquisite' holiday apartments and villas in unusual and interesting foreign destinations at good rates and people paid to rent or to purchase only to find out later that the properties did not exist. She had been successful for many years in avoiding being traced or pursued by those she defrauded through constant rebranding and changes of internet contact details coupled with careful financial planning to hide her assets. None of her publicity was in her own name and none referred to her private address. She quoted a London-based business office that did not exist either.

She may well have continued to act with impunity but, unfortunately for her, two particular customers managed to ensure that she didn't. Neither a senior police officer, nor a top criminal barrister took kindly to being made fools of and made it their business to track her down and bring a case against her. Retrieving people's lost money was a much more complicated process, but the authorities were still hoping to use 'proceeds of crime' provision to seize some of her assets. This being a means by which the police can take and sell assets if they can be proved to have been bought from money acquired through crime.

Surprisingly, many of her friends were still taken in by her and she was assured a hero's welcome in some quarters once she was liberated from her 'terrible ordeal', as they saw it. Rory found fraudsters particularly difficult to work with as they were often so confident and on the surface so convincing that they believed their own deception. Sarah had managed to pass through her sentence without a note of acknowledgement of responsibility, regret or remorse. She had manipulated the system to ensure early allocation to an open prison, where she had successfully persuaded most of the prisoners and some of the staff of her innocence. She had secured a cosy job as assistant to the chaplain, who thought she was wonderful. She had never taken to Rory as he refused to embrace her deceit. As far as he was concerned, the court had got it right and she would serve out the conditions of her licence like anyone else, including reporting to the probation office along with the all the other various local miscreants.

The biggest risk with fraudsters, Rory reckoned, was not spotting their attempts to re-engage with their usual activities, and that would be difficult to combat. Licence conditions, however, did include certain restrictions on her financial arrangements. He hoped that would be enough to either deter her or to expose her if she was brazen enough to commit further fraud.

Early indications of how Karl Pritchard was adjusting to his sentence were not encouraging. Having done relatively well on remand, he was now struggling with the realities of serving his sentence. Unfortunately, one of the other prisoners on his wing instantly recognised him and identified him as an easy target. As a consequence, the bullying had started and he was already bowing under the pressure. Sadly, Rory knew that this was a fact of prison life, but the likes of Karl were not well-equipped to deal with the much harder and more ruthless prisoners that they would inevitably come across. Some would simply say that is the price you pay, he thought, but we don't aim to send people to prison to be brutalised. He felt that reform flounders in such circumstances, which can be counter-productive, a facet he had seen many times.

Rory thought that he would need to visit him soon, whilst he was placed at HMP Birmingham, but could move at any time. Managing the sentence would be a joint effort and Karl would need a lot of support. Returning to his family wasn't a viable option as they had had enough and had effectively rejected him. Only a specialist hostel would take him and those places were rare, although there was one such hostel in Birmingham. After that, some form of voluntary or charitable project may offer an alternative.

Rory thought that he would at least ring Birmingham and get an up-to-date picture. Eventually, he got through to the wing manager where Karl was being held.

'Hi, I'm Rory Scott, probation officer for Karl Pritchard. I understand that he is struggling?'

'Yes, he's struggling. I'm Wayne Turner, wing manager. He and many others, I'm afraid. Karl was unfortunately targeted by the other prisoners as soon as he arrived. We are waiting for a place to become available so that we can move him to the Vulnerable Prisoner Unit. It's mostly full of sex offenders, but there are others like Karl.'

'What are you doing for him in the meantime?' asked Rory.

'All staff are aware. So far, we think that he has avoided taking drugs and is keeping the bullies at bay by doing favours. If the situation deteriorates, we will monitor him more closely and can put him on suicide watch if necessary.'

'OK. Thanks. I will come to see him soon. Is he likely to move from you, do you think?'

'Yes, they usually do. He'll probably go to a more long-term category B prison.'

'Dovegate, do you think?' asked Rory.

'Possibly.'

'When?'

'Whenever, I'm afraid.'

'OK, thanks.'

Rory thought he would book next week to visit Birmingham, if Karl was still there. Restrictions on funding for prison visits were getting ever tighter, but he felt confident that he could secure authority to travel.

Chapter Four

Elis Howell was born at home with the midwife and Aunt Megan in attendance on the January 1st, 1987. He was 8 lbs 3 oz and a healthy boy. Bron coped well, initially, but soon tired of the routine and commitment of being a lone parent. She hadn't realised how much work was involved and how dependent a child was. This undoubtedly felt like the most demanding experience of her life and she was struggling to meet the challenge. She had expected her child to make her feel loved, but it wasn't like that and she worried that she simply hadn't got it in her to give him all the love that he perhaps needed. Aunt Megan was very patient and supportive, though. *Thank goodness*, she thought. She knew that she would not have coped without her.

In time, Bron found some work cleaning and managed to place Elis in a nursery with social services support and further help from Aunt Megan. The social worker seemed very keen on the idea, she thought. Elis did seem to do well at the nursery, she had to accept.

It wasn't long before she caught the eye of a new man and fell pregnant for a second time. Afan Howell was born the following year after a difficult birth and was always a sickly child. By the time he was born, his father had long since made his excuses and moved on. Bron hadn't got the energy to chase him and didn't see him again. She accepted it. She could survive. She felt stronger the second time and still had Aunt Megan to help her.

Bron didn't ponder on why her relationships seemed to fail. Her experience as a child of her parents' relationship, and social interaction in general, had not equipped her well for adult life. Sadly, however, she lacked the perception to understand and interpret these events and seemed destined to blindly carry on in the same vein. She just seemed fatally attracted to the wrong sort of men – to the ones who would always love her and leave her.

Aunt Megan could see the reality and it saddened her, but she felt powerless to change it. She felt that she had done her best to assist and advise Bronwen and to instil some basic notions of good childcare.

After the birth of Afan, she considered that she had fulfilled her duty to assist Bronwen and it was time for both of them to reassert their independence. She managed to broker an arrangement with the family for Bron to return to Porthmadog and for her to secure council accommodation. Aunt Megan couldn't persuade Bron's father to talk to her, but Bron had heard from a friend that a boy she was at school with would like to see her again. She had agreed to meet him when she arrived back in Porthmadog. Aunt Megan hoped against expectation that this new prospect for Bron would turn out better than her previous attempts at creating any stability in her life.

Headlong, Bron soon embraced the fantasy that a new man in her life would provide all she needed. They soon formed a new relationship and, in time, Glyn Morgan fathered her third child, Rhys. He was a strong and healthy child from birth and progressed well through his early years whilst his father popped in and out of their life as it suited him. Bron was never really sure what he did for a living, although he never seemed short of money. She had asked him, but he was always evasive. Bron was conscious that the great days of Welsh mass employment in heavy industries like coal and steel were long gone. Slate exporting and ship building, once prominent in the area, had also fallen into decline many years ago. She assumed he must work in the tourist trade in some way, like many people in the area did.

Glyn was a natural drifter. He came from a travelling family background and was used to moving around. He had learnt some dubious ways of making money from an early age and was used to switching from one dodgy deal to another. 'Keep moving and they won't catch you,' he always said. The thought of any notion of commitment to a partner, or to a stable or static lifestyle, was completely alien to him. He paid little attention to Rhys but no more or less than to Elis and Afan. He felt that he more than paid his share in supporting the family, especially considering that two of the three boys weren't his. Oddly, he quite liked the attention he got, particularly from Elis, when he did call in or spend any time with Bron.

Bronwen continued to struggle as the boys grew up. Life was chaotic, money was always tight and Bron constantly felt on the edge. Eviction was threatened many times, with Glyn usually saving the day with a last-minute payment. Bron supplemented her benefits with some short term cash-in-hand work, dabbling in stolen goods and occasional casual prostitution when she was desperate.

The boys learnt to survive from an early age. Elis could appear to be distant, deep and private, or to engineer being the centre of attention. He had the ability to usually persuade people to do as he wished. Afan seemed unable to cope and Rhys was the most capable. Perhaps he learned from his brothers' mistakes. The local school persevered with all three boys, with exclusion being avoided on more than one occasion.

Elis was always in trouble for fighting, stealing or unruly behaviour; he didn't seem to relate well to other children, and he seemed to find it easy to tell lies when it suited him. He was good at it and could be quite convincing until it became apparent that it was pure fabrication. Afan was withdrawn, distant, unkempt and disorganised. Rhys was always the smart one. He was bright and knew how to use his intelligence to his own advantage.

As the boys progressed through education, everyone knew the Howell brothers. Elis always had a gang around him, so no one messed with him. He protected Afan. Rhys used the family reputation when it suited him and distanced himself from it when it didn't. Elis idolised

Glyn, who he referred to as his father. For the most part, Glyn seemed to relate reasonably well to him.

Social services, the youth service, health and education welfare were all heavily involved in the family throughout the 1980s and 1990s until all the cuts came and services started to be withdrawn. The agencies tried hard to keep the boys on the straight and narrow and to avoid some of the obvious pitfalls, but it was difficult. Being drawn into crime, debt, struggling to make relationships were recurring features of their lives. Hanging around with other similar youngsters and older dubious influences came all too easily to them, particularly after Glyn went through a period of repeat short-term imprisonment and the boys, especially Elis, missed him terribly. Elis worshiped him and tried to copy him, which was, in fairness, despite Glyn's attempts to persuade him not to.

Youth court and supervision followed for both Elis and Afan, although Rhys was smart enough to avoid it, at least at first.

Elis was an early candidate for the area court diversion scheme. This was a multi-agency exercise to identify at risk children and attempt to engage with them early to prevent them drifting into further trouble. Elis was well known to the local police from about the age of nine for unruly behaviour – theft of anything that could raise a few pounds for sweets or cigarettes, and for chasing cats with his dog Mutt. Glyn had brought the dog home unexpectedly one Christmas. Mutt was a cross breed and fell just outside the official definition of a dangerous dog, but he was trouble nevertheless. Elis learnt to use him for status and intimidation. Other local kids complained of being stopped and forced to hand over comics, sweets and any small change while the dog stared menacingly as it sat at Elis's side. Agencies all attempted to instil more pro-social values, a sense of respect for others and a sense of responsibility in all three boys, but it was hard in the face of being constantly undermined by anti-social messages from home.

Elis took Afan out with him when it suited him and blatantly used him for his own convenience, although Afan thought otherwise. Afan thought that they were on equal terms and failed to see that he was being taken advantage of.

More formal police and court proceedings seemed inevitable.

Chapter Five

Emma was starting to create a plan for her future. She considered several options and undertook some basic research before coming to the conclusion that it was time to move on from large-scale corporate business. She felt that her various contacts could potentially be useful to her. Her ambition was to help others succeed. She wanted to establish her own consultancy business to advise small and medium size enterprises or, indeed, those looking to start up a new business. She was excited by the prospect. It also had the potential advantage of being able to work from home. That could make it easier to establish a new home with Rory around mid-Staffordshire without the need to consider access to Birmingham on a daily basis.

They had started looking around in the villages near Church Eaton and Wheaton Aston, east of Upper Lowbridge. There weren't that many properties available at first until they saw something interesting.

'Rory, look I've found an advert for the sale of an old school at Coppermere, where we got married!' announced Emma.

'OK. Let me have a look.' said Rory looking at the advert. 'Sale by auction, I see. It obviously wants some work doing to it, but that's fine. Guide price £180,000. That's great, I've never been to a house auction before, have you?' he asked.

'No, I haven't, but I've got a feeling I'm going to! I would expect a lot of interest though; a rural property with scope for improvement. I wonder if it has outline planning permission?'

'That could work for us, Emma. There's room for an office/study for you. It may have some land with it too?'

'Not at that price, Rory.'

They made their enquiries and the property was said to be in reasonable condition with planning permission for conversion to a dwelling house. There was also an option of renting a small piece of land attached. The village apparently had a lively community, All Saints church and a pub called The Stag Inn. They quickly decided that it was worth a look and set off to drive to Coppermere the next day.

The manor house that they had used for their wedding lay just outside the village and had an interesting history. The local land owner was apparently quite forward-thinking for his era and was one of the people who saw the advantages of educating his work force and providing decent accommodation and some basic health provision. The estate had prospered and specialised in breeding horses. They later became a major supplier of horses to the army during the First World War.

'It's out on the Newport Road towards Church Eaton, then simply follow the signs,' said Rory, trying to remember the route after Emma had elected to drive.

They drove through the countryside, excited at the prospect of just the sort of project that they were looking for. As they entered the village the area looked appealing; they saw the church on the right and the stretch of water from which the name was presumably derived. It seemed to be lined by copper beech trees.

'Look, there it is!' said Emma, pointing ahead.

'Oh yes, there's a sign saying sale by auction in two weeks' time,' replied Rory.

They parked the car and walked up to the lot. It was a classic Victorian school building with a high arched front porch entrance. The windows were high and impressive but would all need to be replaced. The basic frame of the building seemed solid enough, but the interior would need completely refitting. The property sat on quite a large plot with scope for different approaches to utilising the space. The setting in the heart of the village they considered to be an advantage, close to the pub and the church and embedded in the community. They both instantly loved it.

'Oh Rory, it's lovely. I want it. I just want it, whatever it costs. We can do this!'

'Yes, but it's well beyond a DIY project, Emma. This will need an extensive renovation team. We would probably need to spend as much again as the sale price and it might well sell at beyond the guide price. It would be a stretch, but I agree it's a wonderful prospect as a long-term family home.'

'That's it then, Rory. We have to buy it,' said Emma with her usual decisive confidence.

Rory was not so sure but could see that Emma was dead set on it.

***

In his prison cell, Glyn was thinking. He remembered one day that he had come home when expected. He remembered that the house was unusually calm. The children were all in bed. There was no dinner prepared. Bronwen was crying.

He remembered asking her what the matter was. He probably didn't express much sympathy. He recalled clearly what she had to tell him. She had said that Rhys had come home from school that day and looked her in the face and asked why it was so hard for them and so easy for others, why others had nice clothes and went on holidays. She said it broke her heart. Rhys was only five years old.

'Mummy,' he had said, 'why do you always look so tired?'

She couldn't answer him and couldn't hide her feelings. She had sent them all to bed with no tea so that they didn't have to see her cry. 'When will this end?' she had asked him. 'Why don't you stay for more than a few days at a time? Why can't we do better?'

Locked in his cell, it had struck home; it hurt. Had he done his best for her? No, if he was being honest with himself. He had taken on Elis and Afan, though, neither of whom were his birth children. His dealing did take him away sometimes, but she never complained about the money or asked where it came from. Maybe money was not enough? She seemed to waste most of it anyway, and not on the kids.

Will I do better when I am released from prison this time? he asked himself. Well, that was the question, and he was absolutely sure that he didn't know the answer.

Chapter Six

Emma was excited. Rory had promised to take her away for the weekend to Snowdonia. Emma was quite adventurous but wasn't familiar with the mountains of North Wales. Rory had persuaded her to camp on the first night and to attempt a short walk in the area the following day. He had carefully planned the trip, hoping to entice her interest and not to put her off. Fortunately, the weather was good for late summer and they set off in good spirits on Friday evening after work.

They drove down towards Wolverhampton, taking the M54 towards Shrewsbury. Even on a Friday evening this was a relatively clear route, allowing for reasonable progress before reaching the smaller country roads later. As they skirted around Shrewsbury, they talked with anticipation about their weekend to come. It felt good to get away and, now that they were married, it was nice to know that weekends didn't have to end with the sadness of parting!

The road through to Welshpool and Newtown was reasonable but quite slow due to the occasional agricultural vehicle. Opportunities to overtake safely were limited and Rory had to just bide his time before moving swiftly past a tractor.

They began to climb as they took the narrow road through the hills up towards Beddgelert. This was an attractive run. After a good journey, they arrived at the Cae Du campsite just outside Beddgelert village before dark.

The site was well organised and set up for walkers and families, making it clear that party animals were not welcome. Music and excess noise were strongly discouraged. Facilities were good and the grounds were well kept. The standard of campsites varied so much, Rory thought, but this one was in good condition, with no areas being waterlogged or boggy.

Areas were subdivided into sections and named using letters of the alphabet for ease of recognition. They had selected area F and Rory quickly pitched the small tent that he had borrowed from a friend. Emma stood by and watched as Rory pretended to know exactly what he was doing but did manage to erect and pitch a tent that looked reasonably competent. He was relieved that it seemed intact and had all the necessary components, including plenty of pegs. He had brought a blow-up double mattress and good quality sleeping bags so felt confident that Emma would not be cold.

They arranged their kit quickly and set off down the path by the river to the town to find somewhere to eat. Beddgelert looked charming, with its compact rows of cottages, the river and the mountain scenery in the background. At the end of the path, there was an inviting-looking pub on the left and they managed to find a table. The bar area was not too busy and felt welcoming, the food was good and the service quick, which was just what they needed in the circumstances after a long week at work and the journey they had taken.

Walking back to the tent in the dark, Rory had remembered to slip his head torch into his pocket, much to Emma's relief. The tent felt cold but they soon snuggled into their sleeping bags and thought of the prospects of good weather and a nice walk to come. It was an exciting time, with warm memories of the wedding and thoughts of the school house and the prospect of setting up their own home together.

The following morning, the sun was shining as forecast and the views were already spectacular when they first opened the tent. Sharing a small tent is intimate at the best of times, which for newlyweds was also romantic and exciting. Rory wanted to continue to demonstrate his camping skills by rustling up a cooked breakfast on his compact gas stove. Emma was amused more than impressed, but they both enjoyed the breakfast anyway.

Rory was excited about what was to come and described his planned route to Emma, who stoically showed an interest. Rory had worked out a route from the campsite that followed some old industrial workings and a modest climb to a view point then a gentle descent to Llyn Dinas and back to the campsite.

'There have been many accidents here over the years, Em. The ground can be steep and slippery, so be careful,' remarked Rory.

'Wasn't there a story about a school party that visited here? I seem to remember hearing about it at the time. It was quite a news story.'

'Yes, I think so, but I can't remember the details,' replied Rory.

'That's right. Wasn't there some sort of inquiry and someone got into trouble over it?'

'Yes, I think you're right – that's what usually happens.'

They walked on, enjoying each other's company and sharing their aspirations for the future. The route wasn't too long so Rory had estimated well and achieved his goal of giving Emma a good introductory experience. They returned to the campsite in the early afternoon and walked down to the town for tea and cakes.

It didn't take long to pack up the tent and set off for Criccieth to stay over Saturday night. Rory had found a nice little farm bed and breakfast not far from the town. It was a pleasant drive through the forest area to Porthmadog, where they stopped for a brief wander on the beach at Black Rock Sands.

The sea was out some distance, leaving a clean wide expanse of sand to walk over. Dogs ran freely and cars were allowed to drive across the beach. A big 4x4 set off confidently, followed by the more tentative dash of a little Fiesta that nearly lost its exhaust crossing a fast-flowing water channel.

They walked hand in hand towards Criccieth Castle, enjoying the view and just being together. There was a fresh sea breeze, which was pleasant. Rory looked on with pride as Emma's hair blew in the wind over her face, making an attractive image in the sunlight.

The weather remained warm and bright and time was on their side so they set off towards Pwlleli and Abersoch. There was a large holiday park on the outskirts of the town, which for many years was run by Butlins. This is now under new ownership and still remains a popular holiday destination, with caravan sites dotted along the coast. Abersoch, however, caters more for the surfing and sailing fraternity. They found the small town to be full of designer shops and nice places to eat. It was good to see somewhere doing well. The harbour was quaint and the town pleasant to walk around. Unlike the older-style coastal towns, this was busy with people bustling along everywhere.

It was the first visit to the Llyn Peninsular for both of them and they instantly liked it. Rory could remember going on a school trip as a boy camping in Snowdonia but didn't think that he had been back since. He wondered why but could not think of any particular reason, just that he was pleased he had decided to return.

Returning back along the coast road allowed more time to think about the school house and its potential should they be lucky enough to be able to buy it. Rory knew how much Emma was taken by the place and he really liked it too. As they drove along, life felt good, contented, promising and exciting.

They soon approached Criccieth and found the farm where Rory had booked a bed and breakfast. The family were very friendly, made them some tea and showed them their room. It was predominantly a sheep farm and their two young children were very happy to tell them all about it and show them round. They talked confidently, obviously being used to guests, and introduced them to the various animals by name. Emma thought that they were enchanting. The children talked about their life on the farm and Emma and Rory enjoyed the family's company and being outdoors in the open air.

When Emma prompted Rory that they had better think about finding somewhere to eat, the farmer's wife offered to accommodate them.

'We do provide an evening meal as well, actually, and you are welcome to eat with us tonight, if you wish? We're having lamb stew and mash.'

'That's very kind, and it sounds lovely,' replied Emma.

After a good meal, and helping read goodnight stories to the children, Emma and Rory retired to bed too. They slept well. A hearty breakfast followed and, after helping feed the lambs, they said their goodbyes and set off towards home. They drove back via Bala to see the lake and Llangollen to stop for fish and chips. A steady run down the A5 through to Shrewsbury and back to the M54 took them home by late afternoon, in time to think about work the following day.

'Thanks Rory for organising that. It was a lovely weekend,' said Emma, leaving Rory feeling pleased and glad that his efforts were appreciated.

Bracken was pleased to see them and, fortunately, had already had his walk. They fussed him for a while. Emma's thoughts drifted back to the school party, the lost child and the condemned teacher. *What had happened to him?* she wondered.

Chapter Seven

The Howell brothers were a constant challenge to the local secondary school. Always in trouble or suspected of some misdemeanour. Elis needed calming down and his energies redirecting, whilst Afan needed to be drawn out of himself and to gain some confidence. Confidence wasn't a problem for Rhys, however. His tutor saw real potential in the lad but feared that it would never be fulfilled. The odds were against him, the temptations too great.

He will probably struggle to shake off his deprived background, his tutor thought. That would probably shape his future, unfortunately, but nevertheless he hoped that Rhys might be able to break free.

He knew that the boys needed to be occupied to keep them out of trouble and, as the head of PE, he tried to involve them in as much sporting activity as possible. Both Elis and Rhys did well in the school rugby teams and Afan could be persuaded to run cross country races. Rugby was a legitimate outlet for youthful masculinity and also helped develop team work, discipline and self-control. The rugby code of respect for the referee was also a useful tool in Mr Evan's armoury to try to counter their unruly and chaotic home life. Cross country for Afan, as an individual rather than a team sport, suited him and gave him a means to combat some of his frustrations. He wasn't particularly good at it but Mr Evans encouraged him and kept him on board nevertheless.

So when the head suggested to Mr Evans at the beginning of the school year in 2002 that it would be a good idea to introduce the brothers to his Duke of Edinburgh Award group, he could hardly refuse. The D of E group at the school was a significant success, giving kids largely from poorer or deprived backgrounds opportunities for self-development. It had been a vehicle to enhance the life chances of many. Not that all the kids appreciated it, or indeed their parents, but Mr Evans was prepared to ride that.

Despite his faith in the scheme, Mr Evans did have reservations. He knew Rhys would cope with it and add something to the group, and he would benefit from it, but he was not so sure about Afan. Elis he knew would be difficult to manage. Elis would want to take over a group, to dominate it rather than lead it. He also had the ability to belittle others and undermine their confidence. Nevertheless, he could see the potential advantages and the Head was dead keen on the idea. Mr Evans could see that it may just divert Elis long enough to keep him in school and avoid exclusion. He calculated that the risks were worth the potential benefits and agreed to take all three on a one day introductory practice hike. The route was to be relatively short, just to give the youngsters a taste of the outdoors and an option to join the scheme at bronze or silver level later.

On the day of the walk, the weather was kind and looked to be stable. The route was from Beddgelert, through the forest, over a modest hill and down to Llyn Dinas, then back along the track to the start point. In total, this would be approximately six kilometres and a comfortable half day. There were some old quarry works along the way, which added the opportunity to learn something about local industrial history.

The group was of mixed ages and included both boys and girls. None of them had done anything like this before and, although the challenge was modest, some of the group were quite anxious. Mr Evans had another member of staff and two volunteers with him, who he had carefully briefed to keep an eye on the Howell brothers. In the event, Rhys rose to the challenge and demonstrated his potential leadership ability. Afan plodded along largely alone, but did seem to enjoy it nevertheless. Mr Evans was pleased that Elis related well to one of the volunteers and actually was quite helpful to some of the others, particularly one of the girls who he had obviously taken a liking too. In short, it was a success.

The Head was pleased and made a point of speaking to the boys, which made a welcome change from their more usual disciplinary encounters. The brothers had something positive to report to their mother when they got home and she was relieved and pleased in equal measure. Another school group regularly went beachcombing at Black Rock Sands, collecting fossils and items of interest together with cleaning away rubbish.

Mr Evans was pleased to see the brothers making an effort to join in, particularly Elis, although he was convinced that his motivation was more to do with being with the girl he fancied. He thought, *I must speak to Rhian Williams's tutor to keep an eye out for her*. He knew that Elis could be a bully and was not used to taking no for an answer. He seemed to remember that Elis's mum had given birth to him at sixteen and he didn't want to risk history repeating itself with another unwanted teenage pregnancy.

The brothers continued to be active with commitments to school sport, the emerging D of E group and various activities organised through social services, the youth service or the youth offending service. *Maybe Elis can keep sufficiently below the radar to avoid the slippery decline into criminality and custody*, hoped Mr Evans. When small numbers dictated the use of combined age teams, their rugby team performed well, with Elis in the front row taking on all comers and Rhys orchestrating the game from number ten. They were a fearsome double act.

Elis soon learnt the basics of how to twist and turn a scrum, how to force the opposition prop to drop his knee and bring the scrum down, giving away a penalty. He learnt how to bully the opposition and throw the odd punch when the referee wasn't looking. He seemed to just like being in control and lacked any real sympathy for anyone else.

In one needle match against a local rival school, the opposition were leading at half time and it was clear that they had several 'star players'. Elis took every opportunity to harass and niggle their best players in an attempt to put them off. He was also learning the dark arts of bending the rules just within breaking point to secure any advantage, particularly in any close encounters. Holding shirts, digging players on the floor and excessive use of elbows were all in his repertoire. He did, however, also have the makings of a fine player, if he could channel his worst excesses. It was also all very effective, as they won the game, much to the delight of his team.

Rugby was a saviour for Elis; a legitimate vehicle to express frustration and to burn excess energy. He loved the physical challenge and the chance to smash the opposition. The PE staff recognised that they were potentially playing with fire but kept a careful eye on his activities in the hope of preventing anything getting out of hand.

The team was quite settled and used to each other's style of play. That was until David Jackson arrived; he was a lad from England who had just moved into the area and had been the team captain at his last school. Elis did not welcome the competition and took a dislike to him. The PE staff could see David's potential and were determined to integrate him into the team. He provided something different and set up a healthy challenge for places in the team.

Most of the boys had started playing at the local club from the age of about eight. At that stage, it was more about having fun and everyone having a go rather than being too competitive but, as they grew, the boys generally wanted to win. They liked the experience of testing themselves against other teams and wanted the coaches to select the best players. By the time there were eleven and twelve, joining secondary school, a competitive spirit was well established and they were quite a successful team. Most of the core of the team joined the same high school, much to the delight of the PE staff.

Regular PE and rugby training after school helped develop their fitness and skills levels. The PE staff liked to concentrate on basic ball handling skills in an attempt to teach them to protect the ball, keep it in play and pass accurately. Rugby had become a fast, athletic game and all players needed to be fit and able to fully enjoy and participate in the game.

When David was first introduced to the team at a training session, it was obvious that Elis was going to take a dislike to him. David played scrum half and was lean, fast and athletic. Elis was not; he was heavy, strong and rough, lacking the finesse of a back. Elis was a natural forward and a pack leader. David was very confident and found it easy to project himself. He spoke clearly and with authority; he was obviously a gifted player but, at the end of the day, he was still English. David was surprised by the reaction he received; he had assumed that his new team mates would readily accept him in due course. Unfortunately for him, he had underestimated the situation.

The rest of the boys didn't like his attitude either. He needed to be more conciliatory in how he presented himself, but no one from the team was going to help him if he carried on like that. On the occasions when Rhys played in the team at fly half, David's presence was going to be even more difficult. Rhys wasn't too concerned but could sense his brother's objections so, on their first game, Rhys joined in Elis's attempts to discredit David at every opportunity. They passed him short ball, they delayed supporting him in the loose and they tripped him up and trod on him all over the field. Then towards to end of the game, which they were winning easily anyway, David messed up the last pass that would have ensured a try under the posts. All the team turned on him and expressed their frustration, disappointment and almost hostility. Poor David, for all his confidence, found the whole game quite a torrid experience and didn't know quite how to handle it.

He simply wasn't expecting, nor had experienced, that level of animosity before.

David didn't help his cause by showing an obvious interest in Rhian. She seemed to respond to his charm, which made it worse. When his advances became known to Elis, fireworks were inevitable. Things came to a head when Elis confronted him one day after school and called him 'an arrogant English bastard'. When David casually responded in kind and called him 'an ignorant Welsh twit' Elis reacted and swung a fist at him catching his left eye. Others managed to intervene to stop things escalating and, after some posturing, the boys went their separate ways.

The following day at school, David was sporting a right shiner and soon everyone knew the story. Mr Evans took it on himself to call the two boys together and order a truce. They reluctantly shook hands and things did seem to calm down between them, at least initially. Elis had made his point and had maintained his status in the group and that was what mattered to him.

Mr Evans did remember to have a word about Rhian Williams and her tutor did try to speak to her about it and did look out for her on their trips to Black Rock Sands. Elis could be a handful and kept on wanting to stay on the beach as the tide came in with the risk of being cut off. Sadly, such accidents were not uncommon on that stretch of coast. He did seem to be attracting Rhian. Rhian was a sensible girl, though, and knew that her father wouldn't approve, but somehow Elis was a fatal attraction.

Mr Evan's new D of E taster group experienced a few more simple walks and started to learn about navigation, camping and clothing and equipment suitable to walk out on the hills. Safety was important and a sense of balance and responsibility were key messages to the influential young people. There was much to learn, but the group did respond with reasonable enthusiasm. David soon grasped the basic principles of the use of map and compass, and Elis envied him but tried not to let his jealously show, at least not to Rhian.

By the autumn term of 2003, Mr Evans felt that his fledglings were ready for something a bit more challenging before he intended to invite them to commit to taking part in the award scheme. He wanted to test their suitability. He chose a route from Rhyd-Ddu car park, skirting around Y Garn to Mynydd Drws-y-coed and across the causeway to the obelisk, with access there and back through the forest. Y Garn was too severe, he reasoned, at this stage with its very steep and narrow ascent. It was potentially too dangerous and risked simply putting the youngsters off.

On the day, conditions were blustery, with the likelihood of some showers later. The group were in good spirits and set off at a lively pace. Mr Evans felt confident that they would cope with it. Afan was always a concern but he felt that the group would carry him along. Elis seemed more than occupied with seeking the company of Rhian, which at least kept him away from antagonising David.

The youngsters were all talking in small groups and moving along briskly without complaint. David was trying to build alliances within the group, but was finding it hard work. Initially, the route left the car park and soon turned into the forest and the start of a steady incline. Elis was bragging to Rhian about his rugby exploits and some of the others tried to take the opportunity to pair off too. Mr Evans pointed out landmarks on the way and took opportunities to reinforce lessons about map reading and navigation out on the ground rather than in the classroom. Elis was still more interested in Rhian until Rhys pulled him away to give the girl a break.

'Hey come on, Elis, give the girl some space. Most girls don't actually share your passion for rugby, you know, or are terribly interested in the intricacies of front row tactics and your scrimmaging technique.'

'What?' said Elis unimpressed. 'She's lapping it up, isn't she?'

'I don't think so, brother.'

'Well, where's your girlfriend then?' was the curt reply.

They continued through the wood and stopped for a drink before starting the steep climb up to Myndd Drws-y-coed. Mr Evans took off a layer of clothing and packed it in his sack. As usual, most of the group were wearing full waterproof gear with several layers of clothing underneath. It often took groups a while to realise how much you sweat if you over dress, and then how you become uncomfortable. This was one of the many skills and routines that the group would need to master to become an effective unit if they were to be ready to go out on the hills on their own. It was always interesting, Mr Evans thought, to see who emerged as the natural leaders and that it was not always the ones you would expect. Over the years, the hills had proved to be a vehicle for some of the quieter youngsters to assert themselves. Leadership took many forms, but in this context, the starting point was being able to navigate. A group soon gained confidence in someone who could guide them to their objective and, equally, would lose confidence in anyone who demonstrated that they couldn't.

The volunteers and the teacher took the opportunity to talk freely to the kids in a less formal atmosphere. It was a rare chance to get to know them better and for the kids equally to see the staff in a different light. The characters came forward; the jokers, the risk takers, and the moaners would all reveal their true colours by the end of the trip, no doubt.

As they battled up the hill in strong wind, the group were beginning to feel the full effects of mountain weather. Much has been written on pacing and time and distance calculations, but it is certainly true that progress in the mountains on rough, steep or uneven ground is slow and that you need to allow extra time for ascent. Thirty minutes per thousand feet was the conventional wisdom, but Mr Evans knew that a novice group could take much longer. However, the group were doing well and keeping together.

Naismith's rule, although devised in the ninetieth century, was still an effective guide, allowing some twelve minutes per kilometre on flat ground. The skill was interpreting the rule to suit the group, which Mr Evans knew, if done effectively, could prove to be a fairly accurate guide to calculating the likely time taken to complete a given route. GPS technology was in its relatively early stages of development and no doubt had its place, he acknowledged, but Mr Evans preferred to put his faith in map and compass. *Using these tools, navigation is as much an art as a science*, he thought. GPS seemed somehow to be cheating, although he could see the advantage of being able to check your grid reference at any given time.

Mastering the skills of navigation was the key to successful mountain craft, Mr Evans always thought, and it is vital to have grasped the basics by the time the groups were allowed to set off on their own. That sense of independence and responsibility was an essential part of the award scheme but had to be balanced against safety considerations. Generally, group leaders would walk along a similar route and be mostly in sight of their youngsters and meet up regularly at pre-arranged check points.

***

Once at the top, the view was spectacular, and below them was the steep stage. To some it looked ominous.

From the top of the hill, they could see straight down to the causeway. It was a narrow strip of land covered in grass that offered a route across the gap between two hills and on to the objective at Mynydd-Tal-y-mignedd, marked by a distinct stone feature. The wind blew strongly across the gap. They could see the coast out in front of them and the Snowdon range behind them, although Snowden itself was, not unusually, covered in cloud.

Mr Evans called the group together and warned them to be careful as the grass was bound to be slippery and the causeway stood on top of a very sharp shelf on both sides. He ordered no one to fall.

The group crossed the obstacle carefully, as instructed, with the two staff front and back and the two volunteers positioned within the group. Some of the girls showed obvious concern and Elis unhelpfully laughed. Even Afan told him to shut up. The grass was slippery, as he had warned, but right up close the causeway was perfectly wide enough to be safe in good conditions, if people were sensible. Having crossed the tricky bit, the group confidently marched up the next hill to the top to stand proudly by the obelisk. Out came all the cameras for happy snaps until Mr Evans warned that the weather was closing in and that they had better move back across the causeway quickly. He drew the group together and counted heads. Where was Elis?

'Anyone seen Elis?' he asked.

'I think he headed off with some toilet paper,' said one of the girls, looking slightly embarrassed as the group either blushed or laughed. By the time Elis had returned, the weather had deteriorated, the cloud was closing in and Mr Evans told them all to put their waterproofs back on.

'What waterproofs?' said Elis as he broke ranks and headed off at speed on his own back along the path towards the crossing, followed promptly by Rhian. Afan and Rhys followed behind as Mr Evans called them back. Recognition dawned that suddenly the situation had changed very quickly and things were now potentially serious. He looked at his fellow member of staff and told her to follow the brothers with one of the volunteers and tell them strictly to WAIT for the rest of the group on the other side before proceeding down the mountain.

By this time the cloud had closed in and rain was lashing down heavily on the remaining members of the group as they stood awaiting further instructions. Mr Evans quickly considered their position: a split group and suddenly critical weather with virtually no visibility and a narrow path to cross with very steep sides and no room for error. Ideally, he knew that he should rope the whole group together so that if anyone slipped the rest of the group would easily be able to stop them falling, but this procedure really needed to be practiced first and there was no time for that. Also he knew that Elis would not want to wait, especially if he hadn't bothered to bring his waterproofs. He had to be decisive, the group were getting cold and some of them were beginning to look frightened.

'Right,' he said, quickly pulling the rope from his rucksack, anticipating its use for reassurance as much as in the interests of safety.

'I need everyone to hold on to this rope to stay together. I'll lead and we'll all walk along the path close to each other. Crouch down low and place your feet carefully. You will be OK,' he said, trying to sound confident.

The group did as they were told and started to move behind him across the narrow gap with him at the front and his volunteer at the rear. Visibility was virtually zero and his head torch was of little use. The group held their discipline and nerve to start with but then the line started to break up and panic set in with a rush to get to other side once the rest of the group became visible.

At least on arrival his colleague had managed to gather in Elis and his brothers, aided helpfully by Rhian, and crucially keep them together. Quickly, Mr Evans packed up the rope and moved off to get down out of the weather and off the hill. The group followed as he passed, a disapproving glare directed at Elis, who by now was soaked to the skin. Fortunately, the route down although steep was fairly straightforward, leading to the edge of the forest and a degree of shelter, at least from the wind.

In the trees, the group gathered and Mr Evans handed Elis a change of top and a spare waterproof jacket from his sack, if only to prevent him from further harm.

It was only then that they became unsure that everyone was accounted for.

After quickly counting heads, Mr Evans declared that they were one person short. The group looked around between themselves until one of them said, 'Where's David?' It quickly became apparent that David, the English boy, was the one who was missing.

Chapter Eight

Emma had done some more research into the old school house at Coppermere and the auction process. Her endeavours indicated that the school had a good history and had only closed ten years ago when the number of children in the village fell below a critical level. The building had been largely left vacant since then. The additional piece of land was two acres of pasture available to rent. It might be nice, she thought, but really did they need it? And what would they do with it? Although she anticipated that Rory would be keen to have it as a dog run cum vegetable garden.

Emma carefully prepared for the auction. Her research led her to believe that the guide price was reasonable. The sale price, however, would be determined by how many serious bidders were there at the auction. The advice was to set a ceiling of how much you were prepared to pay to secure the property and to stick to that and not get carried away on the day. Rory agreed and, given a guide price of £180,000, they thought a ceiling of £200,000 was both reasonable and affordable.

Rory had done some research on local builders and had found a family firm who specialised in old building conversions. The firm had expressed an interest, having been aware of the property for some time. They did say, however, that they wouldn't be surprised if it went for much more than the guide price and that, depending on the extent of any conversion, anywhere between another £150-300,000 plus would be a reasonable estimate of cost.

Reluctantly, therefore, the couple did have to accept that the school house might prove to be out of their price range, but they decided to go to the auction anyway, if only for the experience.

Around the auction room there were cars parked everywhere. The room was full. There were mostly young hopefuls like themselves, several builders and some men in business suits. The auctioneer was curt and drew the gathering to order as Emma whispered in Rory's ear, 'Remember that £200,000 is our limit, but I really want this house, Rory.'

'Ladies and gentlemen, the next lot has generated considerable interest. Today we are offering a rare opportunity to purchase an outstanding old character building in a pleasant village location, with outline planning permission for conversion to a dwelling house.'

The room fell silent, as anticipation mounted.

'Where shall we start? Who will give me £100,000?' invited the auctioneer.

Hands soon went up and bids followed in £10,000 lots as the hopefuls dropped out and the builders competed between themselves. Rory & Emma wisely held their council, not wanting to simply inflate the price. A number of builders shook their heads as the price reached £150,000 and the men in suits started to show an interest. A builder next to Emma had had enough and turned towards her.

'It's always the same, love, the vultures have arrived. That bloke on the left, he's a solicitor, no doubt representing a property speculator who will pay top money then do nothing with it, when young folks like you want somewhere nice to live,' he said as he left chuntering.

The man he had referred to bid £160,000. The other men in suits offered £170,000 then £180,000, then £190,000.

'Now Rory, now,' Emma prodded him.

'New bidder, £200,000. Thank you, sir,' responded the auctioneer.

Some of the men in suits started to look away, but the bidding continued to £210,000. Rory knew what it meant to Emma so bid £220,000, as she smiled at him until the solicitor killed it by bidding £250,000, and smiled smugly. The room breathed in and no one raised a further bid.

'Sold to the gentleman in the blue suit at £250,000,' called the auctioneer as he brought down his gavel.

Chapter Nine

'Take the group back to the car park and the mini bus. Here's the keys, take the kids home. Ring the Head, he'll want to know,' said Mr Evans with authority as he handed the keys over to his young colleague.

'I'll go back to see if I can find him. I'll see you back at school eventually. What colour waterproof jacket was he wearing?' he asked.

'Blue,' replied one of the girls as the tears rolled down her cheeks.

He turned to walk back up the hill into the driving rain and swirling mist. The group watched him go then turned away to trudge back through the forest. They walked in silence. It had been a good day until Elis had spoilt it and now they had lost David. The realistic ones amongst them realised that any fall from that path was going to result in serious injury at best. They were beginning to think that they might have lost him forever.

Deri Evans pressed on with determination with his wife's words ringing in his ears as he had left home that morning. 'Be careful,' she had said, and that was just it – he always was! Thoughts of twenty years of teaching and nearly as many involved in the D of E all ran through his mind. *Is this it?* he asked himself, for he feared the worst and that any subsequent inquiry would inevitably castigate him.

He walked on. There was no point in shouting out, no one would hear and poor visibility meant that he would only see David if he literally bumped into him. *Blue jacket*, he thought. He arrived back to where the group had reformed on the home side of the causeway. There was no obvious sign of anyone, let alone David. *Why had he taken them across?* he accused himself. *The weather was obviously deteriorating. Why hadn't he turned back at that point?*

Deri stood for a while and listened; nothing but the wind, and he tried again, but he could still hear nothing except the whistle of the wind. *Is it safe to cross the path again?* he thought. No, probably not, but he felt that he had no choice; he had to try to find the boy. So, bending low against the strong side wind, he started to edge forward. About a quarter of the way across, he found some marks in the grass. *Skid marks?* he asked himself. *Possibly.* He stopped and examined the area in more detail. He couldn't be sure so he continued across the path to the end and back again without seeing David before concluding that it was time to ring for help. He knew that he needed mountain rescue.

In such circumstances a mobile phone could prove vital, but when needed most they often fail to find a signal. He found some shelter as best he could just off the summit on the home side and delved into his sack to find the rudimentary school safety mobile phone. It was set up for certain numbers (the Head, the local hospital etc.) but of course that wouldn't help him here. He breathed deeply and rang 999. No answer, no signal. He moved about the hill but couldn't get through. There was no alternative; he would have to come down far enough to hopefully make the call.

After a while, he did manage to get through on a poor connection, asking for mountain rescue and logging his basic message. 'A teenage boy wearing a blue jacket is lost on the hill in the area of the obelisk.'

Fortunately, his college had taken the initiative and rung 999 when the group got back to the minibus. She had been able to explain the wider picture and that Deri had gone back to try to find him and that, if he hadn't found him, she anticipated he would go to the bottom of the ridge to check there.

Deri was pretty sure that he had heard an acknowledgement and the reassuring message that a team was on their way. *Unfortunately, the weather is still too poor to deploy the rescue helicopter*, he thought. He made his way back towards Mynydd Drws-y-coed and downhill to the edge of the forest. From there, he turned west on a compass bearing and headed for the bottom of the ridge. If David had fallen, he was likely to have come off on that side and to be at the bottom of the slope. Even if all that speculation proved to be right, Deri was not optimistic for the lad's chances of survival. Such a steep fall at speed over hard rock was bound to be brutal.

As he worked his way around the edge of the forest, the weather started to clear. Strong winds were blowing away the cloud and some visibility was returning. *Maybe the helicopter could make it after all*, he thought. The ground was very steep for landing, however, but within a few hundred metres there was something of a plateau that might be a suitable landing point.

Then, as the cloud lifted, he saw something blue. Deri stopped to gather himself and looked across the landscape at the bottom of the slope. There, towards the near end, was what looked horribly like a piece of blue cloth. It was somewhat ragged and blowing in the wind, but whatever it was covering was not moving.

As he got closer, Deri could hear the sound of a helicopter in the distance. As he approached the blue shape, it became obvious that it was a human body, lying face down and still. He stood, feeling overwhelmed by grief and regret, as he gently rolled the body over to reveal its face.

Yes, despite the injuries, Deri was sure that this was the body of David, a boy from his school, a boy who had only just moved into the area and who was the last of the group to join. In fact, his parents had only signed the consent form yesterday and now their son was surely dead. What a waste of a young life, the loss of this child in his care.

Deri stood, shocked and horrified, as the helicopter approached. The pilot skilfully managed to land as close as he could on relatively even ground. The rotor blades slowed as two people emerged from the side door to meet him.

'Hi, I'm Angus McKay, leader of the local mountain rescue team,' the first man announced, 'and this is John Jones, one of the team.'

Deri recognised him as the local butcher, mountain rescue remaining a service staffed by volunteers. Together the men walked across to the boy as Deri explained a little of the circumstances. They checked him over and, although none of them were medics, they all felt sure that the boy was dead.

'Just to confirm, Deri, you are sure this is the boy who was missing?' asked Angus.

'Yes, I am. It's David, definitely,' he replied.

They returned to the helicopter for a stretcher and, as sensitively as they could, lifted the boy onto it and carried him inside.

'Get in, Deri, we'll need to take him to the hospital first then the family will need to be informed. I suggest that you come with us.'

Deri agreed and climbed aboard. The helicopter quickly took off and eased away across the hills and back to civilisation. Angus looked across at Deri. 'I'm sorry,' he said. 'Whatever happened, sometimes there are no answers. These can be dangerous places and accidents will happen.'

'I'm sure neither the parents nor the authorities will see it that way,' Deri replied quietly.

'No, probably not.'

Chapter Ten

Although they had prepared themselves, the loss of the house at Coppermere was devastating. Emma was really upset, although she did appreciate that Rory had done his best and that there was no way that they could have afforded to carry on bidding beyond £250,000. What really annoyed her was the feeling that the solicitor was almost playing with the rest of the audience and, as the builder had implied, his budget was almost limitless. Also, if the builder was right, and the buyer simply intended to sit on the property with a view to making a killing in the future, that didn't seem fair at all. Emma felt that she wanted to live there, to have children there and contribute to the local community, not just leave a beautiful old building to deteriorate further.

Rory was more pragmatic, arguing that they had learned from the experience and another suitable property would come on the market at some point. It was unlike Emma to be so emotional; she was usually the calm, hard-headed one but this had really got to her. The joy of the wedding, the prospect of a life with Rory and a new business venture on her own were all really exciting, but the loss of the school house had burst the bubble. She sat and cried as Rory tried to comfort her with memories of the honeymoon in the Cape Verde islands.

They had initially planned to visit Sardinia and Corsica, off the Italian coast, but had thought better of it once they realised that the crisis in Syria and North Africa would inevitably mean that the islands could be flooded with desperate migrants. Whilst they both felt sympathy for those people and were disappointed by the meagre response from the international community, they felt that this was not the context that they were looking for a honeymoon. They had considered the Canary Islands until a friend suggested Cape Verde, off the west coast of Africa. Remote, unspoilt and tranquil, more appropriate as a destination for a romantic retreat.

The honeymoon had been magnificent. The Cape Verde islands were beautiful, with lovely beaches and dramatic, rough seas. Given its location, it had a trading history and now depended largely on tourism. The population was largely of North African descent. It had been colonised by the Portuguese and thrived during the years of the slave trade. The population lived mostly a simple life with a relaxed African Mediterranean attitude assisted by a warm and pleasant climate. Most food and basic supplies were shipped in so continuity of supply was dependent on the weather. It was not unusual to run out of things for weeks on end but that seemed to bother the tourists far more than the locals.

They stayed in a small hotel on Sal Rel and travelled between the islands to Santiago, the largest, and the capital Praia. Reading about some of the islands' history was interesting. They also visited Santa Maria and Minelo by boat. Each passage was different, with access to the smaller islands being facilitated largely by the local fishermen. Journeys were short and seemed quite precarious in such small boats but the risk was worth it to experience the true tranquillity of these special isolated places. They enjoyed them all and felt privileged to have had the opportunity.

It was certainly relaxing and a charming place to have stayed for their honeymoon. As couples often do on this landmark occasion, they promised each other that they would return at some point to rekindle the memories. It had been very romantic and was a very special place.

After a while of feeling sad about not securing the old school house, Emma was able to bounce back by throwing her energies into planning her new business career. She liked the idea of independence and felt confident that she could more than survive on her own. It was a new focus, a subtle change of direction, opening new doors and offering promise and potential.

Chapter Eleven

The weather continued to clear as the helicopter landed safely at the hospital. With all due sensitivity, the crew carefully carried the stretcher out of the chopper and into A&E. A medical team were waiting to check the casualty. The mountain rescue volunteers had completed their responsibilities and quietly and efficiently packed up their kit and prepared to leave. Another member of the team had arrived at the hospital to drive them home. Deri said his thanks and goodbyes. He took a moment to gather himself before walking into A&E to hear the inevitable news that the casualty had been declared dead from blunt trauma injury. David was dead. That was it. There was no retrieving the situation now.

Deri braced himself for what was to come. A member of the medical staff sat with him for a few moments and asked what had happened and Deri explained. He described the poor weather, the narrow path the slippery surface… the body wrapped in a blue waterproof at the foot of the slope.

Deri pulled his phone from his pocket to ring his wife. She had already heard. She was shocked, her emotions split between concern for the boy and his family and anxiety about her husband, as he was ultimately responsible for the safety of the group. D of E had been his passion, she knew that. Stretching young people, giving them room to explore for themselves and learning how to cope with risk were all valuable life experiences, but she had always warned him not to leave himself exposed. She feared, quite reasonably, that if there ever was an accident then all the support for the scheme could quickly evaporate. It seemed now that those fears would be realised and she worried about his future. How might he fare under the intense scrutiny that would now surely follow? And what would be the outcome? For now, however, she knew that her role was simply to be there for him.

Deri's next call was to the Head. He liked Neris Jones, one of the new breed of young female head teachers; bright, energetic, determined and much more the manager than the old guard used to be. Running a large secondary school these days, he recognised was a complex undertaking, requiring a far greater breadth of expertise and management skill than hitherto when the expectations and pressures weren't so great and the local authority carried much more of the burden.

'Neris, it's Deri. I'm sorry,' he said, finding it hard to hold back tears.

'Come now, Deri, whilst this is awful, we must keep a sense of perspective and *WE WILL* get through this. The time for inquiry and all that follows is later. For today, we must concentrate on letting people know, supporting all involved and making arrangements for coming together to share our loss. Obviously, the prime focus needs to be on the parents. I rang them as soon as I knew, hoping to avoid them hearing it first from somewhere else. They were numb, as you'd expect – the poor dears.'

'I don't know them. What are they like?' he asked.

'You are aware that David and his family only recently moved into the area. He's taken over as the local fire station commander on promotion and transfer to here from Gloucestershire, so I don't know them either.'

'They will be asked to identify the body, presumably, or at least be invited to see him?'

'Yes, Deri. I expect so,' the Head replied sombrely.

'OK, well, I'll wait to see them then.'

'No Deri, that might not be the best idea; you will not be the person they want to see right now. We need to give them some space. I'll speak to you later,' she said calmly as she rang off.

OK, I'm already persona non grata, he thought to himself.

Still in his mountain kit, with his rucksack on his back, Deri walked out of A&E, wet, tired, hungry and feeling vulnerable, when it occurred to him that he was miles from home and without transport. The prospect of a tedious bus or train journey filled him with dread. As he walked away, a couple were approaching him. The man looked up and spoke.

'Hello, Mr Evans isn't it?' he enquired.

'Yes,' he said, surprised.

'I'm Barry, David's father. Can you tell me what happened?' he asked calmly.

Relieved, Mr Evans replied, 'I'm so sorry. We were on difficult terrain and David must have slipped. I found him at the bottom of a steep slope. I could see then that he was dead. I really am so sorry.'

Deri felt that nothing else needed to be said. As he looked into the man's eyes, Deri could recognise that at this moment this was about two men acknowledging the loss of a son. There was no recrimination, no request for more detail, just a sense of shock and loss.

'We're here to identify our son, Mr Evans. We'd better go in.'

Barry took his wife's hand. She avoided eye contact with Deri as they walked into A&E.

Two police officers were just leaving and they approached him too.

'Mr Evans?'

'Yes.'

'We will need to talk to you about the death of David Jackson. Would you join us in the car please?'

Deri complied, sitting on the back seat with one of the officers. They introduced themselves and started to take some details.

'Where are you going now, sir?' asked the officer next him.

'Home, I hope.' Deri replied.

'You don't look like you're in a fit state to answer too many more questions or take a formal statement now, sir.

We have to return to Porthmadog quickly. How about we run you home, have a chat along the way and get the basic picture? Then we'll come to collect you tomorrow for a formal statement.'

Deri nodded in agreement. He appreciated that they were being more than reasonable and recognised that he really didn't have any choice but to comply with their instructions.

Chapter Twelve

Towards the end of a busy day at work, Rory took a call from Karl Pritchard's mother.

'I'm sorry to bother you, Mr Scott, but I'm worried about my Karl. He's not coping with being in prison. He rang me last night very briefly to ask me to send him money. I said I couldn't. He said that he borrowed a mobile phone to make the call from his cell and the other prisoner charged £10 a minute to use it.'

'I see, Mrs Pritchard. I know he's struggling, but he did commit two nasty street robberies and, if you do that sort of thing, then this is what happens. You end up in prison. He knows what it's like – he's been there before. If you send him money, he will only ask for more. He must avoid getting into debt in the first place,' Rory replied, wondering if he should have been more sympathetic.

'Will they move him, Mr Scott?'

'Probably.'

'You'd let me know, wouldn't you? And you know I can't have him back, not again?'

'Yes, I do and I will let you know if I hear anything about a move.'

That evening, Emma and Rory talked about their next move while walking Bracken along the canal bank. They had tried to put behind them the disappointment of not being able to buy the school house.

'Shall we continue to look in the same area, Rory? Or should we widen the search?' asked Emma.

'Something might come up. We just have to be patient, Em.'

'But I don't do patient, Rory!' she responded.

'I suppose we could explore other areas.'

Rory's phone rang as Bracken bounded back towards him with a stick in his mouth.

'Hello.'

'Mr Scott?'

'Yes.'

'It's Lewis's solicitors, acting for the local authority for the sale of school house in Coppermere. I'm ringing to inform you that the sale has fallen through with the preferred buyer and that I can offer you the option to buy it at your bidding price of £220,000, as the next nearest bidder.'

Emma could see Rory's face light up as he answered, 'Yes, that's marvellous that will be fine!'

'OK, I'll send you a formal offer in the post.'

'Thank you.'

Emma waited eagerly as he put his phone back in his pocket.

'Em, the sale of the old school has fallen through and I think I've just bought it!'

'Wow, that's fantastic!' she replied, enthusiastically throwing her arms around him.

'Fancy dinner at The Old Plough, Em?'

'The Old Plough it is, Rory!'

***

After all the disappointment of the past few weeks, Emma and Rory could look forward again to the future with confidence. Bracken lay down, calmly hoping for some titbits as they sat in the bar and tucked into the Tuesday 'two steaks and a bottle of wine for £25 deal'.

'Rory, this is fantastic. It's such a beautiful place. I'm really looking forward to it. I've been travelling around for years now and I feel ready to put down some roots,' said Emma, responding to the news about the school house.

'Yes, I'm ready for a place of my own, our own, after years of house sharing – somewhere to make our mark.'

'What do you think about renting the extra piece of land?' asked Emma.

'I think I'd like that, if we can afford it…' he replied.

As Rory was thinking about the process to come, and the size of the project, he could see that Emma was already thinking about carpets and curtains!

Chapter Thirteen

The police arrived the following morning, as promised. Deri had just managed to shower and eat something the previous night before crawling into bed. Although he'd had a long sleep, he still felt tired and the emotional impact was still unfolding. He kissed his wife goodbye as he got into the police car, assuring her that he would be alright.

The officers were the same two men who had brought him home last night and were polite as they made light conversation. At the station, Deri went through all the normal procedures in checking in before being shown into an interview room. He sat down on one side of the table and looked across at the two officers who formally introduced themselves.

'Good morning, Mr Evans. I'm DCI Karen Machin and this is Sergeant Sunni Rashid. Let me start by explaining our interest and intentions here. Firstly, I want to acknowledge the sad loss of David Jackson and the impact on his family and the whole school community. We appreciate the impact on you too but, equally, I'm sure you appreciate our responsibility in trying to establish if there is any criminal culpability arising from David's death. I can tell you that the D of E scheme have launched their own inquiry into the conduct and safety of the events that day, obviously including your part as the party leader and scheme coordinator. Their emphasis, I should imagine, is largely on trying to draw any lessons learnt.'

Deri nodded, as he listened intently.

'We need to take a statement from you of your recollections of the day and particularly the tragic event itself. I'll leave you with my Sergeant initially to do that. Have you any questions?'

'No, but I would like to say that I agree with and accept what you've said and that, as far as I'm concerned, this was an accident. I may be found wanting in how I conducted the day and some of the decisions I made, but I don't feel responsible for David's death.'

'OK,' the DCI replied.

Sunni took down the whole story, from the Head's suggestion to involve the Howell brothers in the scheme, to the introductory walks, and the planning and execution of the day in question. Deri spoke clearly and with confidence in providing a very thorough and full statement.

Sunni then left the room and returned a while later with his DCI.

'Thank you, Mr Evans, for your cooperation. I've read your statement and it provides a very good picture of how you saw events. We need to go away now and interview all the others involved and see where that takes us.'

Deri nodded as he pushed back his chair ready to leave.

'There is one more thing however, Mr Evans...' said DCI Machin.

'Oh yes?' responded Deri, disappointed that the interview wasn't over.

'There is the matter of the allegation against you.'

'What?' Deri replied sharply in disbelief. 'What allegation?'

'The allegation that is of inappropriate behaviour towards one of the girls in the party.'

'I beg your pardon?' replied Mr Evans, immediately feeling angry and confused.

'Rhian Williams has alleged that you made inappropriate remarks to her, made her feel uncomfortable in your presence and placed your hands on her buttocks as she attempted to scramble up a steep section of rock. If proven, Mr Evans, that could lead to criminal charges against you. We are yet to take full statements from Rhian and other members of the group so we will need to come back to you on this matter.'

Deri's head dropped, he felt confused and crestfallen. *What else could happen?* he asked himself.

Officers started the process of interviewing all those involved, while the school tried to manage the aftermath; the media intrusion, the difficult questions and the soul searching. The family organised the funeral, which was a very sad and moving affair that was well attended by the whole community. The community came together to acknowledge the loss of a family who were new to their town, to share their grief and to support each other in the immediate period following the incident.

The Head consulted with the chair of governors. This was difficult territory, but in the circumstances, having given it due consideration and taken advice, they felt that they had to come to the obvious conclusion about how to respond.

Back home, Deri took a call.

'Hi Deri, it's Neris from the school.'

'I was expecting a call.'

'Deri, I'm sorry but in the circumstances, and after consultation with the governing body, we have to conclude that your continued presence in the school represents an unacceptable risk to children, so I have a duty to inform you that you are suspended with immediate effect, whilst these matters are investigated.'

This was the message that he expected but didn't want to hear. He had also heard from friends that the D of E inquiry was already raising serious concerns about the conduct of the expedition from an initial reading of the various reports. Deri reflected that this was not looking good.

Deri sat back wondering what to make of it all. Suddenly his world had imploded. He had lost a child on the hills. He was suspended and could face criminal prosecution. Whatever happened, he knew that his career was in tatters and that things were never going to be the same again.

His wife, Marion, returned from doing some shopping and could instantly see that something had upset Deri, as if he didn't already face enough difficulty.

'What's happened, love?' she asked. 'You look awful.'

'I've been suspended.'

'Oh.'

'I expected it.'

'Really?'

'Yes, they don't have any choice, it's just how the procedures are set up these days, but it doesn't feel very nice or indeed very fair. I feel like my head's in the noose from the onset.'

'What do you mean?' Marion asked, concerned.

'Well, someone has to take the blame, carry the can, and usually those who make that decision ensure that it isn't them,' Deri replied calmly.

'Yes, but surely there's a process; you make representations and an independent body decides?' posed Marion in both hope and expectation.

'Well, not exactly. Yes, I'll get my say, but it feels like the odds are stacked up against me. The decision-makers are hardly independent, love; it's the head and the governors. If you were them, would you take responsibility, as a policy failure or for lack of support or whatever, would you blame the person doing the job?'

'Oh, I see,' she replied.

'And in a sense, I deserve criticism. I never should have chosen that route or I should have turned back, but at the time I felt that the kids were up to the challenge. That will no doubt be torn apart by the D of E inquiry.'

'Aren't you being too hard on yourself and a bit negative and cynical, love?' Marion said, trying to ease his sense of guilt.

'No, I'm being realistic,' Deri replied.

Deri hadn't even mentioned the sexual allegation – he couldn't work it out. What was that about? He wouldn't act like that and he didn't act as described. *Why would Rhian make such an allegation?* he wondered.

Chapter Fourteen

In the immediate aftermath of David's death, the local community was tense. Rumours spread like wildfire about Mr Evans, with questions being asked about other staff's behaviour. However, people were good to David's parents, welcomed them into the community with an open heart and helped them as best they could.

Even on reflection, the funeral remained a very sad and subdued affair in people's memories. Members of the community continued to do their best to try to support David's family. Many heartfelt feelings of loss were expressed to Mr and Mrs Jackson over the weeks following the funeral, with acknowledgement of the sense of David's unfulfilled potential. It was a bitter blow to anyone but having just arrived in Porthmadog seemed to make it worse with the loss of close support from family and friends that they had left behind in Gloucestershire.

The other pupils involved in the incident mostly wanted to move on, for all the questioning to stop and to be able to get on with their lives. They tried to pull together but there were tensions.

The Howell brothers inevitably reacted in different ways. Rhys coped relatively well and stood apart from the endless analysis, buckled down to his school work and dared to dream about his future. He was determined to break out. Not to be held back in the suffocating self-perpetuating grip of his failing family and a hard core of others like them in the town. Not to accept his lot, not to cast blame on everyone else, feel angry, hit back and bear the inevitable retribution. No, he was clear in his mind that such thoughts and feelings were not for him. He looked to a future beyond Porthmadog. In the old days when ships regularly took hopefuls to the promise of a new life free from poverty in America and the new world, Rhys would have been one of the first to volunteer to jump on board. *What is the equivalent in the modern world?* he asked himself, and the best he could come up with was education. That was his route out. That was his route to a new beginning, somewhere else, anywhere, but not here.

Afan struggled. He looked to Elis for inspiration but found little support forthcoming. His moods had become deeper, his introspection more intense. Afan was stealing, he was cheating and, most significantly, he was drifting and his mental health was deteriorating as a consequence.

Elis didn't care about the inquiry. He cared about himself and the fact that he wanted Rhian. He enjoyed adding fuel to the fire in denigrating Mr Evans. He enjoyed the return of his total leadership of the rugby team now David was no longer around and behind the scenes he bullied, he intimidated and he built his position of dominance, encouraged by his father, Glyn Morgan, and unseen by his mother Bronwen.

Living hand to mouth could lead to a permanent feeling of being on edge, of anxiety and insecurity. The lack of a basic domestic routine at home and lack of stability and nurture tended to instil a fear of chaos and a need for self-preservation. The professionals might have referred to it as a lack of attachment, the bonding between parent and child that instils love, security and nurture. Without that experience, forming meaningful relationships in later life becomes so much more difficult. The essential elements of trust and respect amongst others are missing and can be irretrievable. With mother struggling and Glyn's casual attitude to fulfilling any kind of consistent role as a stand-in father, the Howell brothers were largely left to make their own way, without guidance, support, encouragement or sanction. Any positive role models had to be found elsewhere. Rhys was more than capable of making such links, of understanding the context that life had handed him, but his two brothers didn't find that so easy.

Elis knew that Rhian's father didn't like him and didn't trust him; this was not surprising once Elis became aware that he was a police officer. Elis knew all the local bobbies, or rather they all knew him, but he hadn't met a certain DC Williams before he started chasing Rhian. Rhian's father was a specialist. He worked in child protection, helping to monitor the local pimps and trying to prevent young girls being drawn into prostitution.

Her father was not impressed when he found out about Elis, but he was more than enraged when he heard from his daughter about Mr Evans, a man a young person should have been able to trust, a man who should have had integrity, and that was unforgivable in his eyes.

Rhian had tried to persuade her father that Elis had tried to protect her. In the end he had conceded but warned her, his words still ringing in her ears, 'OK, Rhian, you see Elis Howell as you seem determined to do so, but just be careful, my girl. The likes of Elis Howell are bad news. He will always be bad news, but you need to find that out for yourself. He may have helped you but only because it suited him. Don't come crying to me when it all goes sour.' She knew that he meant it. She hoped that he was wrong. She knew that she had to be careful.

***

Behind the scenes, Rhian's father brought what influence he could muster to advance a case that somehow Elis was to blame for David's death. He was happy to see Mr Evans swing for it too, but wanted the system to take Elis down with him. The Howell family were well known in Porthmadog and there was little community sympathy towards them in any event, certainly no sympathy from the police who would have been more than happy to see Elis taken off the streets. Rhian's father therefore gained considerable support when he expressed his views to colleagues and more senior staff, who he hoped may have had some influence over the situation.

The police had interviewed all of the D of E group and the staff. The statements were fairly consistent. DCI Karen Machin sat down with her sergeant to review the evidence.

'Let's have a look what we've got. I'll try to summarise; listen and tell me if you agree or if you can add anything. The youngsters seem to be saying that they had faith in Mr Evans initially, up until the point that they crossed the causeway. They do seem to agree that maybe they shouldn't have gone. Then they all blame Elis for splitting the group. After that, in the initial confusion, no one claims to have seen David actually fall off the edge. They all agree that it wasn't until later that the group leaders established that David was missing.'

'Yes, I agree, ma'am, but there are some inconsistencies too.'

'Go on.'

'Well, two of them think that the Howell brothers returned over the causeway to meet the rest of the party and three of them said it was obvious that David was missing well before they stopped lower down and counted heads. Now why would that be?' replied her sergeant.

'Maybe Mr Evans was more concerned about getting the group down the mountain and out of the wind and rain? Remember that Elis wasn't wearing waterproof clothing.'

'Yes, possibly. That could be reasonable.'

She paused. 'In those circumstances, as the group leader, surely you'd ensure that you had everyone with you before you moved off, though, wouldn't you?' concluded the DCI.

They pondered.

'Looking at the staff statements, there are some references to tensions between David and Elis during the walk. Otherwise, they largely seem to endorse the actions taken by Mr Evans.'

'Elis has tensions with everyone, though, ma'am,' responded her faithful sergeant.

'Yes, that's true.'

DCI Machin continued, 'OK, turning to Rhian's allegations, I'm not sure what to make of this. No one claims to have witnessed hands on buttocks but two of the girls say that they witnessed Rhian looking uncomfortable several times during the day when Mr Evans was standing too close to her. There's no history of complaint, allegations or charges against him and nothing on file of this nature relating to that school over the past five years. True or not, I'm not sure that we have enough to make this stick. He denies it and the other staff back him up.'

'OK, so that doesn't take us very far with the allegation but the unexplained death is still an open case, surely ma'am?'

'Yes, I agree.'

***

Some colleagues tried to support Deri and advised him to seek professional help. He did contact the local union regional officer but didn't find him to be very helpful. He pressed the union to offer him a solicitor to advise him and help him fight his case, but initially the request fell on deaf ears.

When the D of E inquiry report was published, the conclusions were damning. The choice of route was severely criticised, the decision to cross the causeway when the weather was deteriorating, the loss of control of the group at a critical moment, the failure to check equipment or practice certain drills in advance, *AND THE CRITICAL FAILURE TO ESTABLISH THE NUMBER PRESENT BEFORE LEAVING THE CAUSEWAY,* were all highlighted as contributory factors leading to the accident.

Although Mr Evans had a good safety record over many years, the inquiry was adamant that he should take no further part in running the scheme. Nor should Elis Howell continue to participate for his actions in separating from the group.

Chapter Fifteen

Deri was distraught, his worst fears realised as he read the D of E report. He accepted some of the criticism but still felt that it lacked balance and that he had been hung out to dry. As he was acting in the name of the school at the time, he knew that he also faced their disciplinary procedures and that, having been suspended, there was now no chance of him being reinstated. Marion tried to comfort him. Some friends and colleagues rallied round but, at the end of the day, Deri felt isolated and abandoned.

It was then that it started. The media pressure ramped up. Reporters from the national press gathered outside his house and a media campaign against him gained momentum. He wasn't safe to walk through the streets. He was effectively a prisoner locked in his own house. Marion found it difficult too. She tried to carry on as near normal as possible but felt the gaze of indignation as she went about her daily business. She had been given compassionate leave from work but that wouldn't last forever. People crossed the street to avoid her, some of the local shops would no longer serve her and she feared answering her own phone.

***

'Barry, look at this. I've found the report of the D of E inquiry into David's death online.'

Horror grew on both their faces as Barry and Julie sat and read through the report, holding hands and trying to concentrate through the tears.

'Poor kid, poor, poor kid, let down by those who should have protected him. They never should have been there! Someone has to be held responsible, somebody has to be held to account!' shouted Barry to his wife as he started to pace up and down.

As an experienced firefighter, Barry was more than familiar with safety procedures and responsibilities in difficult and testing circumstances. He had taken part, led and commanded many incidents where lives were at stake and he knew how close the margins could be sometimes. He sympathised with the view that youngsters deserved the opportunity to experience a sense of adventure in contrast to their ever more wrapped up lives, but he couldn't accept that it was wise or appropriate to expose a group of relative novices to such a level of risk with such little preparation. His son had real potential; he was bright, able, energetic, empathetic and ambitious. He was a leader, the captain of his old school rugby team. He was his son, but more than that, he represented a life unfinished, a life unfulfilled.

After the tears came the recriminations and a lust for action. The Jacksons made contact with their local MP, who was supportive. In the wider context of the attention of broadly what might be called 'middle class crime', there was some public and media enthusiasm for seeing greater sentences and harsher punishments for professionals who fell short of their responsibilities and where lives were lost. Many a family also felt aggrieved to see paltry sentences handed down to those who had killed by dangerous driving. This was similar – no harm was intended but harm had been caused by reckless behaviour. The pressure mounted, some people wanted blood, others wanted what they perceived as justice and others just yearned for greater consistency. However, it seemed that no one was expressing support, or crying out for leniency.

In the corridors of power at Westminster, the debate continued with strong representations from the Tory right to enable and encourage courts to take a harder line on these types of incidents and to hold those responsible to account. The media coverage largely agreed and mostly ignored the counter argument about risk as a balancing act and the need to support the large number of volunteers who gave their time to organise activities for young people. At least some of those in power could see the dangers in going too far and finding a dearth of willing volunteers. If that was to happen, it could only disadvantage young people further and deny them opportunities to broaden their experience.

***

Neris and her team of senior staff, together with the chair of governors, had to consider their response to what was known so far. She had convened a meeting.

'Welcome everybody. Firstly, thank you to all of you for your support and consideration over the past few months; the events have tested us all. Thank you for how you have responded to the need to support our pupils and their families. I'm proud of you all. However, the task is not yet over. We must turn our attention to what actions we see fit to take in respect of Mr Evans. I have spoken to Karen Machin, the local DCI, the members of the local authority and the wider trust and this is how I see our position.

'Mr Evans is formally suspended, as you know, but we can't leave that in place indefinitely. In the interests of all concerned, there needs to be an outcome here. You have all had the opportunity to read the D of E report, Mr Evans's statement and legal and procedural advice that I circulated earlier. Friends, I think our duty is clear here. I propose that we should formally instigate dismissal proceedings against Mr Evans for gross misconduct. I am prepared to listen to what you may have to say.'

A silence fell across the room. Deri Evans had been well liked and respected; no one had expected or wished these circumstances to unfold but there was a sense of the inevitable. No one sought to challenge the Head's proposal.

Deri was informed in writing of the school's intension and advised of his rights of representation. No one official saw fit to contact him in person. Over the space of the preceding few months, his band of loyal supporters had diminished; some had changed their minds, others had fallen away. Some, however, did sustain their support for a colleague. The union was less than helpful. *Why had he paid his subscription for all these years?* he wondered.

The tension mounted for Deri as due deliberations slowly ran their course. He found that his scope to influence the whole process was minimal and no one offered to help him attempt to engage with it. No, Deri felt alone and abandoned while he awaited the outcome, an outcome that he never doubted would be to his detriment.

One mistake, one day of exercising poor judgement, I had never disputed any of that, he thought, *but what of all the successful days?* What of all the young people whose lives had been enhanced by involvement in the outdoor activities that Deri and his team had made available to them? Where was any sense of balance in this judgement? There would be none, he concluded. He had been the leader of the party and a boy had died and he therefore must take responsibility, it seemed. Although no one actually saw him fall, no one could actually determine why or how it had happened, but it seemed to Deri that, despite the presence of doubt, that certainty had been assumed.

After due course and process, Deri Evans was dismissed from his teaching post for gross misconduct. His salary stopped, his pension affected, his career over, his life placed on hold.

The time came when the police finally made contact and Deri felt very vulnerable. Two officers formally came to collect him on a day that his wife happened to be out. He left the house, locked the door and didn't turn back, not knowing what might happen. He was interviewed over several hours under caution.

DCI Karen Machin entered the room in the late afternoon and sat down opposite him.

'Deri Evans, no formal action will be taken against you in respect of the allegations of inappropriate behaviour made by Rhian Williams, but I must warn you that the information will remain on file and may be used against you in the future.'

She continued, 'However, in respect of the death of David Jackson, I am charging you with manslaughter…'

The other words failed to register as Deri crumpled, holding his face into his hands and said nothing. He had opted not to call a solicitor throughout the process, maybe that had been a mistake, he considered, and surely he should now.

'You will appear before local magistrates in the morning, when the Crown will request a remand in custody.'

She paused and looked at him and turned off the tape machine.

'Off the record, Mr Evans, I strongly advise you to seek legal advice at this point and I thank you for your cooperation throughout this inquiry.'

Deri nodded as she got up and left the room to speak to her sergeant.

'Sergeant, ring Cerys Roberts of Hughes, Roberts and Unwin. She's the best defence solicitor we have in the town. Invite her to come in to see Mr Evans please. Tell him it's standard procedure and she's the duty solicitor today.'

'OK, ma'am,' he replied crisply.

Sitting in the interview room, they left a broken man. Feeling very isolated and vulnerable, Deri wondered what the future would hold now. He didn't feel optimistic.

***

Elis Howell opened his letter from the school, in relation to the D of E group. He was informed that he was no longer a member. He laughed, screwed it up and threw it in the fire.

Chapter Sixteen

Emma was starting to make some progress in her transition from business executive to independent business woman. The firm that she had worked for were supportive, indeed enthusiastic. Her proposals were complementary to theirs and presented no threat to their business so they were pleased to help. She was starting to think about a business title, logos, business cards, advertising and building a client base. It was already quite fun!

She let the solicitor know that the school house purchase was back on and Rory spoke to the builder about a site visit and generating some ideas and more accurate costs for conversion. *Will I need an architect?* he speculated. He'd ask the builder.

Rory managed to nip out from work to meet the builder, Gary Cartwright, on site the same afternoon, as he was going to be in the area collecting some materials for another job. He seemed a very genuine sort of bloke.

They arrived together, shook hands and looked along the site towards the building. Rory sensed that Gary wasn't into chitchat.

'Hi, Rory. Now then, the extent and quality of the refit will depend on how much you are prepared to spend and, indeed, how much you are prepared to do yourselves,' declared Gary.

'OK, we hadn't really thought of that, neither of us have any particular expertise,' replied Rory.

'Oh, don't worry, neither have most people, but at least you recognise it! There are plenty of relatively unskilled tasks that you could do to help keep the costs down.'

'I'll bear that in mind. Will I need an architect?' posed Rory naively.

'Now that is a way of spending serious money! You will need some basic plans drawn up yes, to satisfy the council planning regulations and to give me a guide to work to, but I can put you in touch with people who do that. If you want a basic start – secure the roof, the exterior walls and windows, then fit electrics and plumbing, a kitchen, bathroom, internal walls and doors – I'm sure that we can do something that won't break the bank, but remember when you get inside, don't expect to find anything much that will be useable. It will need gutting and starting again and that is where the graft starts. Also, if you are looking for a long-term family home, it doesn't all have to be done at once, you can do it in phases over time, but you will need to establish it as liveable in first.'

'That's really helpful. Thank you.'

'No problem. I have two sons and a daughter all starting out, so I know what it can be like. See if you can get the keys, Rory, and we'll have a closer look inside and then draw up some ideas. Right, I need to move on.'

'Yes, and so do I,' replied Rory.

***

Deri appeared before the magistrates the following morning and was formally committed to Crown Court for trial or sentence. No pleas were taken at this stage. In all the circumstances, the bench did accept an application for bail as there was no evidence to suggest that Mr Evans would do anything other than co-operate fully with the authorities.

Deri wanted bail; he still didn't consider that he was responsible directly for the boy's death and was prepared to fight to clear his name. A remand in custody from the start would have made that much more difficult. The initial bail conditions were stringent but he could live with that. He was to abide by a curfew overnight, guarantee surety of £10,000 and report to the police every day. Being at home meant that he could support his wife and see his solicitor while trying to keep the media interest at bay. None of that was going to be easy, he speculated, but he was determined to comply and make the best of the opportunity.

***

When Rhian finally plucked up enough courage to inform her father that she was pregnant, it came as no surprise. He had warned her. He was nevertheless disappointed and scathing in his condemnation. He wanted to keep it quiet and, without any debate, quickly arranged for a private abortion. Rhian didn't argue, she knew there was no point. She was fifteen and didn't want the baby anyway. The news was contained, a front of respectability maintained, another piece of evidence to damn Elis Howell secured.

***

Deri had several meetings with his solicitor. Cerys Roberts was a local girl and Deri could remember teaching her at school. She had done well, was something of a star pupil, and it was no surprise to anyone to see her launch a successful career.

Cerys had read the evidence and the prosecution case in the advance disclosure. She went through the detail with him.

'OK, Mr Evans, let's go through this,' she said, remembering him as head of PE.

'I think it's Deri now, Cerys.'

'OK,' she replied, feeling slightly embarrassed.

'Firstly, there is no doubt that David Jackson died on the mountain, in all likelihood as a result of a fall from the causeway. Secondly, you were in charge of the party and they were all children. You made certain decisions which the D of E inquiry has exposed as questionable. Thirdly, no one actually saw David go over the edge, so some doubt remains about exactly what happened. Then comes the rub. The prosecution alleges that, as the identified adult, you are responsible in law for his death, effectively through negligence. It doesn't meet the test for murder but that's why they are presenting a case for manslaughter.'

'I see.'

'That's the nub of it really. Am I correct in thinking that you accept responsibility for leading the party and for some poor judgment but maintain that the death was nevertheless an accident?'

'Yes, that's right. How do you think it will go?'

'If you elect for trial, you mean?'

'Yes, I've no intention of pleading guilty!' he replied.

'Deri, it's an arguable case; it could go either way. It will really depend on the sympathies of the jury. The law can only go so far – at the end of the day, it's a judgement.'

'So it would be appealable?'

'Well, let's get the first stage over. So you want to elect for trial?'

'Yes Cerys, definitely.'

***

The local media seemed to be split in support of one side or the other. The national debate had widened to encompass some of the core issues. One side arguing that regulation needed to be tighter to ensure greater levels of safety to protect children and rigour in holding people to account when things went wrong and mistakes were made. The opposite camp felt that children needed exposure to risk and that, in order to deliver the benefits of that experience, the public had to accept a certain level of failure (i.e. accidents will happen).

A spokesman from the British Mountaineering Council issued a statement saying, 'Every year people die on our mountains, in some cases they are wholly ill-prepared, poorly equipped or lack sufficient experience to face the conditions they place themselves in. However, if we want well-led and properly supervised activities to enjoy our magnificent mountains then it's no good automatically castigating the expedition leader if things go wrong. It has to be a joint responsibility with the participants and their parents in the case of children, based on consent and a realistic acceptance of the risks involved.'

Chapter Seventeen

ES Consulting seemed to hit the mark. *Not terribly original but it fits the bill*, she thought. Emma was making headway with attracting some interest from some of the small companies that she had worked with. Not large pieces of work but opportunities to build a reputation. Companies were looking for innovation and, typically, in a small firm everyone was so busy with their nose to the grindstone that they had too little time to plan or to research. So Emma could fill that gap for them; distinct pieces of time-limited work to generate some ideas for expansion, scoping and calculating some initial indication of the likely costs.

The printers were designing some ideas for logos and another friend was working on creating a website and ideas for publicity via social media. Emma was energised by the feelings of excitement generated by taking control, by trusting in her own abilities, yet being conscious of the risks involved. She knew that she had to make it work; failure was not an option – the financial implications would be crippling. After all, she would have a mortgage to pay!

What she really needed now was some more space; the flat simply wasn't big enough to also act as an office, but it would have to do for now.

Rory had managed to persuade the local authority's solicitor to lend him the keys to the school house for a more detailed look around with the builder. Then they would need to talk to the bank again to finalise details of the mortgage that they required, but for today the keys were the next step.

Rory met Gary on site early the following morning, diverting from their usual routes to work. Rory felt quite excited as he opened the front door through the porch way and into the building. The school had closed some ten years ago apparently and had been left unused since then, other than on the odd occasion. Pupil numbers had dropped and cost cutting had forced closure despite quite a vigorous campaign from the local village community.

The interior broadly consisted of a reception area, some offices then a central corridor with four classrooms running off it, leading on to a school hall and some kitchens.

'It's not too bad actually, Rory. Better than I expected. The wooden block flooring seems OK and might even polish up nicely, and most of the internal walls are sound. I can't really make a judgement on the roof from here but there are no obvious signs of water damage so it should be basically OK,' declared Gary.

'Great, so what would you suggest?'

'Well there's lots of scope. I'd say bring your wife down here and just try to imagine a basic layout, how you want the rooms configured, ideally incorporating as much existing internal structure as possible. Both to keep the cost down and to keep the building standing,' suggested Gary.

'OK, that sounds sensible.'

'Early indications are good though, Rory. I'll email some names of people who do plans locally, ones I've worked with who are reliable, then contact me again when your plans are approved and you have the mortgage finally in place. Then we can look again in more detail and estimate some outline costs. OK?'

'That sounds great to me, Gary. Thanks,' concluded Rory decisively, feeling confident in his choice of builder.

***

On the day of the trial, Deri understandably felt tense. He felt that he had little control of the situation and knew that the outcome lay principally in the hands of others. All that he could do was to retain a stance of honesty and try to convince the jury as best he could that he was ultimately not responsible. He didn't feel confident that either the task would be easy or that the outcome would be in his favour.

Deri met his barrister and went through the case again with her. She was business-like. Deri appreciated the process involved in a trial, that of an adversarial approach with each side trying to present their best case and to discredit the opposition.

Each witness was called in turn and the basic facts of the case were reviewed and established. No new angles emerged. The issues remained as Cerys had outlined them; there was uncertainty about how exactly David had come to fall down the mountain and therefore there were different views of who, if anyone, was responsible for his death.

When it came to exploring the precise events on the causeway, it was evident that there was some confusion and some sense of panic within the group. The weather was poor, visibility was very limited and there was little space to manoeuvre. Questioning took a similar form with several witnesses.

'Did you actually see David coming back across the causeway?' the prosecution barrister asked Rhian.

'No, because I was at the front of the group and he was at the back.'

'Did you see him emerge from the causeway when you arrived at the near side?'

'No.'

'So, to be clear, Rhian, you did not see David Jackson alive either on the journey back across the causeway or when the group re-formed on the near side?'

'That's right,' replied Rhian, wondering what he was getting at.

'So, ladies and gentlemen of the jury, I suggest to you that there is no precise verification of how David came to fall.'

The following day, it was time for Deri to be called to give evidence and to be cross-examined. The prosecution barrister had already established Deri's role in the events and had made much of the critical comment for the D of E inquiry.

Deri had been held in custody during the trial. The court fell silent in anticipation as the prisoner was produced. He looked around the courtroom at the sea of faces, hoping to see some indication of support, but none was evident. He looked up into the public gallery and caught a brief glimmer of his wife's eyes.

Questioning took a slow and predictable course, until it became more intrusive.

'Mr Evans, have you read the D of E inquiry report?'

'Yes, sir,' he replied, trying to sound confident.

'And do you accept its contents?'

'I accept that it represents their view and understanding of events.'

'It is quite critical of you, isn't it? Do you accept that criticism?' the barrister asked pointedly.

'I have never denied that I regret some of the decisions I made on that day and I accept that the report was highly critical. I accept it as a view from a respected body making an independent judgement of the events. However, such a judgement, in retrospect, is entirely different from making decisions on the day in the difficult circumstances and conditions that we found ourselves in,' Deri replied carefully.

'Yes, but surely, Mr Evans, the point here is that you should never have led this inexperienced party of young people into those very conditions that you describe, should you?'

'The route was challenging, I accept that, maybe even inappropriate but at the point we first crossed the causeway the weather and prevailing conditions were in my judgement safe. I had no control of what happened afterwards, that the weather deteriorated so quickly; that is in the nature of activities in mountainous conditions.'

'So are you suggesting that the risk was acceptable, Mr Evans?'

Deri's council objected to this statement as a leading question and the Judge invited the prosecution barrister to rephrase it, but the damage was done.

The barrister continued, 'Your honour, was it reasonable, as the leader of this particular party, to expose the group to the level of risk inherent to that particular area of Snowdonia at that time of year?'

Mr Evans paused and the court drew breath. 'I felt so at the time, yes.'

'And how do you view it now?'

'With the benefit of hindsight, I wish I had not used that route.'

'I see. Can you explain to the court what training the group had received and instruction on how to deal with certain situations that might arise in a mountain environment?' posed the barrister.

'We cover basic map reading and navigation, first aid and advice on personal clothing and equipment to be used in the mountains before and during any period of outdoor activity.'

'And rope work?'

'No not necessarily at this stage.'

'So, was it reasonable to expect the group to respond to your instructions to use a rope as a safety line in a crisis?'

'I would have preferred to rope the group together properly in a well-established procedure, but they were not familiar with that technique. I reasoned that this was not the time to attempt to teach them, so I compromised in using the rope as a safety line, as you put it, more for re-assurance than anything,' Deri explained, knowing that it left him vulnerable.

'So can you confirm to the court that handling a rope in this manner would not prevent anyone from falling over the cliff?' the barrister asked firmly.

'No, it would not, but it would provide a guide, a sense of direction and a means of trying to keep the group together.'

'But it didn't work did it, Mr Evans?' concluded the prosecution barrister rhetorically as a decisive hammer blow.

***

When it came to the turn of the defence barrister, some ground was retrieved. She was able to establish from the witnesses that Deri Evans was generally well liked and respected. The parents had been properly informed of his intentions and invited to sign consent forms. The D of E activity in the school had been established for many years without serious incident.

The weather at the start of the day was clear and good for the time of year. The party were in good spirits and the route as far as the causeway had not presented any particular difficulties.

Mr Evans was questioned on his own training and experience and suitability to lead groups in such circumstances, also on his understanding of navigation, mountain craft and of safety and accident procedures.

'Mr Evans, I suggest that it is beyond reasonable doubt that you were suitably qualified and experienced to lead the D of E activities in the school. Neither is this disputed in the inquiry report. Turning to events on the return across the causeway, can you account for how the group came to split at such a vital moment?'

'The group had worked well together until the point when Elis Howell decided to run back across the causeway on his own and his two brothers chose to follow him. I shouted for them to stop, but they didn't. I was then faced with a split group, as you say, at a critical moment. So, initially, I sent one of the volunteers with the second member of staff across the causeway to join them in order to supervise the sub-group and keep them together at that spot, on the near side of the causeway.'

'Did the actions of Elis Howell and his brothers, in your view, in any way contribute to the risk to the remaining members of the party?'

'Yes.'

'Can you elaborate?' the barrister suggested.

'It created a sense of doubt and uncertainty, you could feel it. I needed to seize the moment quickly or risk losing control of the group. That was when I decided to deploy the compromise idea of using the rope as a guide line, in order to restore some confidence.'

'While this is not an established technique, it was an improvisation on your part?'

'Yes, I thought so and it critically didn't take long to instigate avoiding leaving the two separate groups standing and waiting,' Deri replied feeling that they were achieving some sense of understanding from the jury.

'And that would have been a problem if you had elected to use the more conventional technique of roping your group together?'

'Yes, that is correct,' concluded Deri, confidently.

'So you managed to lead your part of the group back across the causeway in the most challenging of conditions and unite the group on the near side?'

'Yes, I did,' Deri replied.

'Can you explain to the court how you came to establish that one member of the group was missing?'

The court listened intently to this highly pertinent question.

'Once we were reunited, my priority was to get the group down the mountain as quickly and safely as possible and away from the worst of the exposure to wind and rain. Once I had done that, we stopped. I checked that everyone was OK, lent Elis some spare waterproofs – as he evidently had not brought his – and then, once I'd counted heads, the doubt emerged whether every member of the group was accounted for. Looking round amongst themselves, it was the group who identified that it was David who was missing. It's easy to miscount in these circumstances, when you are wet and cold, but we counted again several times and it became clear that we were one member short and that David was the one who was missing.'

'Would it have made any difference if you had managed to establish that at the near side of the causeway instead of later someway back down the mountain?' his barrister asked as the court listened intently.

'No, I don't think so. My intention would have been the same: to secure the safety of the group and then go back to search for David. Once we had established that he was missing, there was minimal delay before conducting a search and finding his body. I had to balance that against ensuring the safety of the rest of the group,' Deri responded.

'And can you confirm to the court that it was you who made the call to the police and the mountain rescue service and that it was you who guided them in to the site of the casualty?'

'Yes, I did,' he replied sombrely.

The defence barrister went on to describe how Deri had accompanied the rescue team to the hospital and how he had cooperated fully with the D of E inquiry and the police investigation. In fact, the investigating police officer had commented that she had never known such a well-behaved and cooperative prisoner.

As the case concluded and closing statements were invited, it seemed clear, as it had from the onset, that the case would hinge on whether the jury were convinced that Mr Evans's actions were reasonable or negligent.

David's parents were entitled to submit a victim statement describing how they felt and how their loss had affected them. Such statements are inevitably highly emotive and can be powerful in swaying a jury either way. Mr and Mrs Jackson described in their written statement just how devastating their loss had been of a son so young and with so much promise. They did go on to describe their feelings towards Mr Evans, both in terms of a lack of personal animosity and having a great deal of respect for anyone willing to give so much of their free time to engage young people, but also of the need for people to be held to account when things went wrong.

Finally, the Judge gave the jury some legal guidance as they left the court to consider their verdict, whilst all other parties simply had to wait for the outcome of their deliberations.

The public gallery was full with David's family, members of the local community and Deri's supporters. Glances were exchanged but no words spoken between them. The court professionals hovered around and talked amongst themselves whilst the press eagerly anticipated some drama, however the outcome unfolded.

The jury failed to reach a verdict by the end of the first day and were directed to stay overnight and reconvene in the morning. Eventually, they were in a position to indicate that they had reached a satisfactory conclusion by late afternoon and the court was called back into session. After much consideration, the jury finally came to a majority verdict of ten to two, rather than a unanimous decision.

The Judge looked down and formally asked the foreman of the jury to confirm that they had reached a verdict in respect of the charge of the manslaughter of David Jackson. A polite nod preceded the invitation to declare their verdict.

The foreman rose to his feet, cleared his throat and answered, 'Guilty, Your Honour.'

Gasps rung around the court as David's family celebrated and Marion looked across the court to her husband and saw the sense of shock and disbelief on his face. Calm resumed for the Judge to announce that sentencing would follow in the morning and, with that, the court started to clear as Deri was taken down to the cells for the night for the first time as a convicted prisoner.

The following morning, the court gathered after the previous day's drama. There seemed to be a mixed reaction to the finding of guilt, with sympathy and support for both sides in equal measure. For David's family, this was officially the end of the process. After surely seeing Mr Evans being sent away to prison, they could get on with their lives. For Marion and Deri, on the other hand, the involvement of officialdom had only just started. Prison, probation, and restrictions on employment all lay ahead in a way that they could not possibly have conceived at the time. This would leave an indelible scar. Every job application, every form for official use – passports, dealings with the bank, membership of any organisation – all would ask about previous convictions and could raise concerns about risk to children. Disclosing this embarrassing episode would be a feature of their lives for many years to come.

The court rose as the Judge appeared from his chambers, after the customary shuffling and coughing silence emerged coupled with a sense of eager anticipation. The Judge traditionally made comments at this stage, summarising the case and explaining in brief the rationale behind his sentencing decision.

Deri appeared from the cells to stand in the dock facing the Judge.

The Judge looked down at the court and spoke clearly.

'Firstly, I want to thank the ladies and gentlemen of the jury, whose task is now over and all the staff involved in this case. I offer my sincere condolences to the parents and family of David Jackson and to all others affected by his death.

'The court has delivered a verdict of guilty and it is my duty to pass sentence. I take into account the relevant legal framework, the D of E inquiry report and the findings in court. This is a tragic case with the loss of a young life, the loss of a youth who clearly had much to offer the world and much to live for. There is no suggestion that the defendant actively sought David Jackson harm – on the contrary, Mr Evans had a good record over many years of leading D of E activities with young people – but on this occasion his actions were found wanting; the critical choice of route for a group of novices, the lack of preparation and training for what they might encounter, the loss of control of the group at a critical point and the delay in establishing that David was missing. The use of the rope as what has been referred to as a safety line was criticised by the inquiry as being ineffective and possibly offering a false sense of security. It could also have lost vital minutes that could have contributed to the eventual outcome. In all these regards, Deri Evans, you were negligent and fell short of the standard of supervision that the public have a right to expect in these circumstances when they trust you with the wellbeing of their children.

'I take into account your previous good record, good character and the exemplary way in which you have conducted yourself throughout these proceedings, but I have to conclude that a custodial sentence is inevitable. Deri Evans, for the offence of manslaughter, I sentence you to six years imprisonment. Take him down.'

On that bleak day in early 2005, Deri was led away to start his sentence, as the gasps from around the court intensified. Gasps acknowledging leniency and gasps expressing anything from surprise to outrage. It was immediately clear that this was going to be a controversial decision. Outside the court, the press waited and the police made their usual statement incorporating the views of the family – but, in the circumstances, comments were muted. It gave a sense that, after the finding of guilt, that justice had not really been done, given the relatively short sentence imposed.

The press were left to make of it what they would and the debate about risks and benefits of structured outdoor activity continued.

Chapter Eighteen

In the aftermath, Mr and Mrs Jackson felt cheated. They were not vindictive people and had expressed some sympathy towards Mr Evans, but six years for loss of a life seemed derisory, particularly once it was explained to them that this usually meant serving only three years in custody followed by a period on licence in the community. How could that be right, they argued, when they knew that they would suffer for much longer than that? They felt that, after all the process and proceedings, to end like this seemed an insult to David and gave them no sense of justice.

For Mr and Mrs Evans, the emotions were inevitably very different. Marion feared for how the community might react and whether she would ever be safe again in the town. Deri just hung his head in shame, thinking that after a lifetime in teaching and organising activities with young people that his career and involvement should end like this. Yes, he felt passionately for David and his family, but he still didn't feel ultimately responsible for his death. He accepted what the Judge had said, but that still didn't mean he sent him over the cliff. *It was an accident, surely*, he thought, *an accident pure and simple.*

***

Once matters had had an opportunity to settle, there was an appeal by the CPS arguing that, considering all the circumstances, the sentence was felt to be too lenient. It was explained to Mr and Mrs Jackson that this was a relatively new mechanism whereby the state can apply to review its own sentencing if it was felt to be less than warranted. After all, the defence have always been able to do the same if the sentence was perceived to be too harsh.

In due course, an appeal found in agreement with the CPS and the sentence was extended to nine years.

Deri was informed in prison. He supposed that he wasn't really surprised but nevertheless bitterly disappointed. Not only did this mean another two years in custody, but it made any attempt at appeal on his part more difficult. The legal advice he received argued that he could only appeal in the light of new evidence, simply to say that the court had got it wrong and that he was innocent wasn't going to get him anywhere. Deri felt that he had no choice but to lick his wounds. He was a confident and resilient person, despite all that had occurred, and he determined to see out his sentence in good faith.

The case had been widely reported and he was known in prison as 'The D of E Killer'. Deri deliberately did not seek vulnerable prisoner status and preferred to be open about who he was and take any flack that came his way as a result. After the initial shock of being in custody, he found that he could cope with the regime, but the single most notable facet of prison life was the sheer boredom and monotony. *What a waste of time and public money*, he thought. He busied himself as best he could by helping other prisoners to learn to read and writing letters for them. As a sportsman, he also found solace in the gym and the gym staff took him under their wing as best they could, involving him in any prison sporting activities that were on offer.

Chapter Nineteen

Emma and Rory were pleased with the progress on the school house purchase and the bank had agreed the mortgage details. They sat on two old desks in the main hall of the school and debated the layout of the building.

'Emma, let's keep it simple. I think it lends itself to keeping the school reception area as the hall, then using the two small offices as a boot/store room and an office for you.'

'Yes, that sounds sensible,' responded Emma positively.

'The four square classrooms could all be bedrooms in time, leaving the main hall as a largely open plan living/dining area with a wood burner in the corner. The old school kitchens are OK as a space to refit with a modern farmhouse-style kitchen and the old pantry could be a utility room/cloakroom.'

'Um, we are being creative today, Rory,' Emma exclaimed. 'How about a mezzanine floor from the main living area, accommodating a master bedroom suite?'

'Yes, that would be nice, but it might have to be phase two. If we go for what I've proposed so far, it would make use of the existing solid internal walls and not involve too much actual building work. As Gary suggested, I could help with the basic clearing of the property and anything else he thinks I could do. We can do our own decorating, so the costs shouldn't run away out of control, Em,' said Rory, trying to be practical.

'OK. What about bathrooms, Rory? You haven't mentioned bathrooms,' Emma responded.

'Good point. I suppose one en-suite and one of the four bedrooms could be a family bathroom instead?'

'OK, you go ahead and talk to the plans guy that Gary recommended. It seems to be coming together nicely,

Rory. I almost feel broody!' She suddenly thought that this was as good a time as ever to confirm their intentions. She asked, 'You would like a family one day, wouldn't you, Rory?' in eager anticipation, already knowing his enthusiasm for family life.

'Oh yes, Emma. Yes, I would.'

The readily agreed consensus added to their sense of satisfaction. After the initial disappointment over losing the school house, to now have secured the property felt all the more special. Already Emma and Rory were feeling very comfortable with their acquisition and the exciting prospect of creating a long-term family home.

***

Back at work, Rory remembered that he had promised to visit Karl Pritchard in prison. He rang Karl's mum first to ask if she had any news.

'Hello, Mrs Pritchard. It's Rory Scott, Karl's probation officer.'

'Oh yes, Mr Scott.'

'I'm going to arrange to visit him but, before I do that, I just thought I'd ring you and ask if you have any news?'

'No, not really. After I wrote back to him saying I wasn't going to send any money, I've not heard from him again. I do speak to the mum of another lad who is in prison with him and her son says Karl's still waiting for a transfer to the VPU.'

'OK, Mrs Pritchard, I'll let you know how I get on.'

Rory rang HMP Birmingham and booked to visit in several days' time. Staff said that a move to the Vulnerable Prisoner Unit was imminent.

Walking Bracken along the canal towpath later, Rory wondered how much he would miss Millfield. He had enjoyed his time living there, and liked the access to the canal walks, but knew that he would love discovering all sorts of new places with Bracken around Coppermere. He hoped that the house sale didn't take much longer so that they could get on with the building work. *It will take a while before it is ready to move into,* he thought.

The man Gary had recommended promised to get some simple outline plans back to him in a couple of weeks along the lines that he had Emma had already discussed. He was confident that he could work from the original school drawings and the sketch that Rory had sent him. Without any major change to the internal walls, and being single storey, he didn't envisage any problems. He agreed to add a mezzanine as a secondary stage and get that agreed while they were submitting plans, even if it proved to be some years before it was constructed. Rory was pleased; things were going well, he thought, and more to the point, he was sure that Emma would be pleased too!

***

Before setting out on the day he was due to visit Rory, he knew from experience that it was wise to ring and check with the prison.

'HMP Birmingham.'

'Rory Scott, probation officer for Karl Pritchard. I'm due to visit him today. I'm just checking that is still OK?'

'Hang on a minute, sir. Karl Pritchard, no he's gone, transferred from here yesterday.'

'To the VPU?'

'No sir, to HMP Garth.'

Good job I rang, thought Rory. He knew that there was no point in asking why, he accepted the fact that the prison system often moved prisoners at short notice, usually for security reasons. *HMP Garth, that's at Leyland in Lancashire, located with HMP Wymott,* he remembered. *OK, I'd better ring them instead*, he thought, *but Karl will need a while to settle in…* Rory rang the probation department in the prison just to establish contact and booked a visit for a fortnight's time. He then rang Karl's mum to let her know.

Rory hoped that Karl would be able to stay at Garth for a while but knew that nobody would give him any guarantees of continuity. Moving that distance away at least gave Karl a chance of breaking free from the bullies and to be able to keep his head down if he was sensible. Rory knew, however, that Karl could be his own worst enemy.

***

The house sale completion went through several months later, after the plans were finalised and approved by the council. Finances would be tight for a while. Emma had put her flat in Birmingham up for sale and had received an acceptable offer, but they would still need to cover rent on Rory's flat and the new mortgage until the school house was ready to move into. Gary the builder said that he could start work in two weeks' time and gave Rory some initial instructions to start clearing the site. Gary had estimated an initial cost to complete the work well within their budget, leaving some money aside for fittings and fixtures and for the unforeseen.

Rory still needed to visit Karl after his initial induction at Garth. In fact, he had lost control in the medical unit and assaulted the doctor when he refused to prescribe the medication Karl was asking for. He had consequently spent some time in the block. Staff had warned Rory that Karl was in no mood to see anyone and there was no point in wasting his time travelling to the prison as Karl would refuse to see him.

OK, thought Rory, *let him sweat it out; that's no way to behave.*

Karl was subsequently awarded added days on his sentence for the assault, which was not a good start. Rory was aware that Karl had never had a proper psychiatric assessment but he wasn't gaining anyone's cooperation by assaulting a member of the medical staff.

Chapter Twenty

It was several years later that Glyn left the area for a while to avoid detection by the authorities. Bron always deteriorated when he wasn't around. Gin was her tipple. Without Glyn there was never much money and most of it went on gin. Elis had taken over some of Glyn's distribution business and was good at it. He liked the idea from the start, when Glyn had offered him an 'apprenticeship' and explained the rules: always get your money, don't trade on anyone else's patch, and don't grass.

Sure, Glyn sold the stuff, but he never used it; that was probably the only piece of good advice he ever gave his family: drugs can make you money but that's it. 'They can also ruin your life, so leave that to others,' he used to say.

It was just after his eighteenth birthday that Afan was sectioned for the first time. He had become agitated and was seen wandering around the estate muttering aloud. He was unkempt and in a poor state. He had stopped taking his medication and wasn't eating well. He'd climbed over the fence one night and slept in the park.

When one of the rangers tried to wake him in the morning, he had assaulted him and been arrested. The police didn't like a 'smelly' in the cells and could see what a state Afan was in so they called the medics and he was eventually sectioned under the Mental Health Act as a potential danger to himself and others. It was his first encounter with psychiatric hospitals.

Elis had been doing well keeping Glyn's distribution business going, but his success attracted unwanted attention from others. He proved not to be as smart as he thought when confronted by another local dealer who had decided that Elis had become too successful and needed taking down a peg or two.

When he met with three men with baseball bats round the back of the estate, Elis did better than they expected in defending himself. He managed to disarm the first man, put him down and take his weapon but, by the end of the fight, Elis was in a mess and the attackers left him in the dust covered in his own blood and missing several teeth. They had left him with some jewellery in his pocket stolen from a local elderly lady the night before after they had broken in knowing that the police would find it on him.

A passing paper boy called 999 and the ambulance crew called the police. When they found the jewellery, they instantly recognised it from a break-in the previous evening and were delighted, not only to recover the goods for the old lady but to have caught Elis Howell red-handed. They knew that they could secure a prison sentence for an offence like this, burglary against a vulnerable victim, and that it would give them and the community a break from Elis Howell's various activities.

The assailants left with Elis's mobile phone and a few pounds in cash from his pockets.

'Good. That's him away for a while then.'

'Yes, I'll tell my gran that she will get her jewellery back from the police. I'll just nip round and drop this phone down the back of her chest of drawers in her bedroom. The police will buy her story that a stranger came to the door and asked her if she needed any gardening work. While he walked her round to the back garden, another guy must have nipped inside and stole the jewellery.'

'Yeah, that will do. Sorted!'

Elis had two broken arms, broken ribs, a smashed nose, a large gash on the side of his head and he urgently needed some dental work. He was battered and bruised. The police interviewed the elderly lady, believed her story, and found the phone in the bedroom. They interviewed Elis with a smile on their faces and he said very little. He denied any involvement in committing the burglary or of any accomplice and said he didn't recognise the men who had attacked him. He reckoned the police had planted the phone themselves, it was all too neat, but he felt powerless to influence the situation. He could see the smug expressions on the faces of the officers and how clever they thought they were and how much they were enjoying this.

'How is Elis getting on, sarg?' enquired the duty inspector. 'I hope he's enjoying our hospitality!'

'The little shit is just fine, sir,' replied the custody sergeant. 'Although he seems less than totally satisfied with the catering arrangements.'

'Oh, that's a shame. It beats gruel though, doesn't it? No manners, some of these people. Have you charged him yet?'

'No, would you like the privilege, sir?'

'It would be my pleasure!'

After a brief period on remand charged with burglary, Elis appeared in Crown Court and met his appointed barrister.

'Good morning, young man. Let's not waste any time here; the evidence against you is unequivocal. I take it you will plead guilty?' said the barrister, getting straight to the point.

'It may be, but I didn't do it.'

'Convince me,' replied the brief with a raised eyebrow.

'You're meant to be on my side! Three dealers attacked me. Turf wars, I guess you'd call it. They planted the jewellery on me and the police planted the phone. That's it,' Elis stated dispassionately.

'It happens, whether or not it did in your case, I don't know, but I'm being realistic here. No jury is going to believe you, you are going down. It's just a question of how long. I'll run a trial, if you really want me to, but you'll lose and the court will be vindictive and increase your sentence. You might as well grin and bear it and plead guilty. Even with your record and burglary of a vulnerable victim, at least there were no threats or violence. I reckon you are looking at between two to four years.'

'OK, let's do that,' replied Elis calmly while seething inside.

Elis was convicted of burglary and sentenced to three years imprisonment. For a man already in plaster and carrying broken ribs, he knew that this was not going to be a pleasant experience.

***

When things had calmed down and Glyn returned home, he was not impressed to find that most of his delivery rounds had been taken over by a rival. He knew the family involved. He and their dad had been at school together so he went to talk to him, hoping to regain some territory. He was fobbed off, however, with a shrug and told 'that's how it is' as the door slammed in his face.

Oh well, he might regret that one day, Glyn thought. *Maybe it's time to go back to pimping or try something else?*

He was getting too old for the 'protection' game – internet fraud was the future but he wasn't any good with computers and all that. *Perhaps go round the garden sheds, talk to the car boot guys and see what sells these days*, he thought.

Later in the pub a bloke was telling him what good money top dog breeds go for if you can catch them in the parks or on the beach. *That was worth a try*, he thought. *Must do something, he said to himself.*

***

Elis was finding it hard to adjust to life in an adult prison. He had experienced several short sentences as a juvenile but this was different. Juveniles were all of a similar age but here he found himself competing with guys with twenty or thirty years of criminal experience behind them.

His injuries from the attack made him very visible and the immediate butt of many a jibe and a joke. Doing the basics for himself was demanding enough, but trying to play the hard man as well was all but impossible. This was new territory for Ellis, being so obviously the underdog, and he didn't like it.

The rub of course was that he hadn't even committed the offence! Taking your punishment like a man was one thing when you'd done it but when you were completely innocent, and also the victim in the case, it didn't do anything for his faith in the system. Other prisoners tried to help and council him that was how it goes sometimes, you take the rough with the smooth, and anyway he should remember all the offences that he'd committed and not got prosecuted for, they told him. Good advice, no doubt, but water off a duck's back to Elis, who was busily harbouring a serious sense of resentment.

Once his plasters could be removed from his arms, things got a little easier, but he had to be careful; broken ribs, he discovered, are painful and take a longer time to heal. Elis was very dismissive about any attempts at rehabilitation. In his case, he took the old-fashioned attitude of 'keep your head down and just get through your sentence'. He had a home to return to and, if his father was still speaking to him, the prospect of earning some easy money.

Paying lip service to prison work and attempts at reform came easy to him. What kept him going though was the thought of retribution. He was determined that those three bastards that had set him up were going to get what they deserved. He lay awake at night thinking about it; how best to pay them back? Elis wasn't bothered about being subtle, about trying to catch them out. No, he just wanted to see them to suffer.

Chapter Twenty-One

Once the mortgage was paid and the sale confirmed, Rory and Emma were free to start work on the old school house. They were feeling excited. They ordered a large skip and started clearing the site of residual rubbish. The plot was quite large and in some state of disrepair. Weeds had grown through the old playground and debris lay all around. Much of the playground was retrievable for car parking and possibly a patio area.

Inside there was a considerable amount of dust and rubbish all through the property. Steadily over their first day they managed to use the wheelbarrow to remove twenty barrowloads from inside the house and to collect a good deal of various piles of rubbish from the outside. They were surprised however just how much rubbish a skip can take!

They sat inside, munching a sandwich at lunchtime, dreaming of what it all might look like when completed. Emma liked the simplicity of the ground floor accommodation and how the house would flow from room to room and area to area. The total living space was big with the main open plan space having loads of scope for creative imagination.

They both liked the idea of two wood burners as a sustainable primary source of heating. The one in the kitchen/utility area would heat the water and some radiator pipes and the one in the main living area would have the capacity to warm most of the house, they hoped.

While they were on site, a succession of neighbours and villagers wandered in to say hello and to introduce themselves to the new residents to be. *It's lovely to feel so welcome*, they thought.

People genuinely seemed pleased that the property had been sold to a young couple who intended making the village their long-term base. They really looked forward to village life and becoming part of a community.

Emma was also looking forward to developing her business from home, and also having some spare time to work on the house. Rory was contented with the prospect of years of DIY and building improvement projects to come. He hadn't much experience of practical skills but was keen to learn. *Many a YouTube video will need to be viewed, demonstrating everything from plumbing to gardening*, he thought.

Once Gary and his team started work, renovations moved on quickly. As he had suggested, his first priority was to check and secure the roof. Fortunately, the structure proved to be in reasonable condition. Replacing all the plumbing and electrics took longer than he had expected and, of course, was more expensive as a consequence. However, the end results were good and worth waiting for, they all agreed. There was no gas in the village, so heating to complement the wood burners would have to be electric. At least that kept it simple, they decided. The plaster work wasn't in too bad a condition so Gary felt that it would be alright to patch repair when all the other fittings were in place.

Most of the flooring, as he had predicted, would polish up nicely in time and would lend itself to the use of rugs rather than fitted carpet. Some interesting original features could be maintained, such as some of the children's cloakroom hooks and possibly a black board or two! Rebuilding chimneys and installing the wood burners was the next priority. Gary had used a supplier in Hilderstone before and they were helpful in meeting their requirements. Chimneys had to be lined and fireplaces knocked out to accommodate the stoves. With a bit of imagination, the stoves looked in keeping with the old school theme, as well as being practical.

New windows were ordered and subsequently delivered ready to be fitted. They had decided to avoid plastic and stay in keeping with the style of the property by using wooden frames, which they would stain rather than paint. Plastic guttering and downpipes however seemed entirely practical.

Carpenters then started to fit old style new skirting board. Some of the door frames and doors were still useable and added character to the building. Then it was the turn of the plumbers to fit the kitchen, the family bathroom and the en-suite, all of which needed to be 'practical and functional rather than over the top and expensive', as Rory put it.

As areas became near to completion, Emma and Rory could start to do the decorating. The priority was to have two double bedrooms up and running and leave the third and the mezzanine for the future.

Progress was really impressive as, one after another, rooms were ready for decorating and occupation. Busily decorating their bedroom at the weekend, it suddenly occurred to Emma and Rory that they could actually start to move in and release their flat for someone else. That would substantially ease the strain on their finances.

When they returned to the flat that evening, they contacted the landlord and gave the required month's notice to move out. This would be quite an end of an era for Rory and a major step forward for Emma towards her idyllic dream of becoming part of a village community.

'The Plough for dinner?' suggested Rory.

'Yes, the Plough it is. We've got nothing in and I don't know about you but I'm knackered!' responded Emma.

'We can take Bracken too. We did really well today and it's starting to take shape. It won't be long before our bedroom is finished, including the shower, and then the kitchen, at least to a usable state.'

'True, I can see you sitting by that fire once the season progresses!' remarked Emma laughing.

'You will be able to think carpets and curtains soon!' he responded as he leaned in to kiss her.

'I love you Rory Scott,' she said.

'I love you too,' he replied, enticing her back into the bedroom for a brief romantic interlude before they set off for the pub.

***

ES Consulting was developing a strong client base and Emma was able to continue to ease her transition from being an employee to being self- employed. She hadn't realised how many small businesses there were out there and how little advice and support was available to them.

Recommendation by word of mouth was far more effective than any glossy advertising campaign that she might have been more used to, and her contacts grew rapidly. She found that businesses liked to network too and she was regularly invited to breakfast meetings to share developments and exchange ideas.

Emma found that she had a rapport with her clients and had direct experience of many of the issues that they raised with her; how to launch a business, the cheapest access to finance, devising a marketing strategy and judging when the time was right to take the risk and expand. She felt confident in offering advice and found it generally to be well-received and regarded as helpful. As well as a sound business head, Emma had an element of warmth about her, which readily endeared her to her clients. She came across as genuinely wanting to help them to achieve their potential.

In advising one young couple, she was able to refine their business concept and improve their marketing strategy. After their first year in business, they were making a range of handmade household accessories. Products like bespoke house number plates, a variety of hooks and display units (tastefully mounted on polished oak), and handmade bowls and plates, and sales were going well. They had started selling their wares at craft fairs but were debating whether to open a shop.

An opportunity came to rent a small industrial unit. It had scope for a shop and workshop combined, so they would be able to take commissions and make their bespoke items on site, ready for immediate sale. It would also allow them to expand their product range. With encouragement from Emma, they decided to take the risk and rent the industrial unit. They felt confident that they could make it work. For the future, Emma suggested that they might start to investigate developing a web-based sales platform. This could potentially open up access to a much wider market, but it would need production and distribution provision to be in place if it was to meet that extra demand.

Another couple had set up a dog walking business. They had invested in a large van and had land adjoining their house where they could give the dogs a run. They found an expanding market for not only collecting and walking dogs but for driving around letting dogs out into their own gardens for a brief run and to relieve themselves, as dogs do. The next stage was to decide whether to open kennels to add to their range of services.

Emma generally found that her clients were committed to the plans that they had devised together and usually went on to implement them. They often said that her encouragement and coaching was the element that gave them the confidence to take the risk, move on and achieve their goals. Emma was pleased with her clients' feedback as it was precisely the personal connection and sense of achievement that she was looking for.

She enjoyed the personal contact inherent in her new role and found that she could still do some freelance work with her old firm as and when she wished to. They seemed happy to assign her specific projects that didn't justify creating full-time posts. The arrangement suited them both well.

As her own business grew, Emma continued to grapple with a whole range of new issues. Being an independent entity, rather than part of an existing company, also brought with it responsibility for VAT registration, a need for public indemnity insurance, consideration of resilience and cover for holidays, sickness and out of hours contact, not to mention her own pension arrangements. She found that she had to pace herself and frame her expectations realistically in addressing all of these issues, but steadily and over a longer period of time than perhaps she had first envisaged.

**

As they started to move into the old school house, Emma set up her office as they had originally envisaged in a small room off the hall at the front of the building. It would have been the original head teacher's office. Emma didn't need many facilities; broadband for her computer, a printer and some filing space seemed to complement her favourite old desk and chair quite nicely. She enjoyed being based at home and was excited by the prospect of self-employment and the flexibility that it would offer her.

She had never seriously thought about having children until recently, preferring to be a career woman. Still, she had warmed to the idea and allowed herself to imagine the patter of tiny feet in the house, and the comfort granted her children by being nurtured and brought up in an old school.

As she started to hang some pictures in her new office, a piece of plaster began to crumble as she hammered in a nail, and a whole section broke away revealing the edge of a recess behind it. On closer inspection, it was obvious that the plaster had been used to cover over the area at some point and had boxed in an existing wooden cupboard. Emma eagerly pulled away the remaining pieces of old plaster to expose a full-size built-in cupboard standing proudly in the recess.

Carefully, and with some anxious anticipation, Emma opened the doors of the cupboard. Inside she found shelves and a collection of old school records. As she lifted them out carefully, she found a positive treasure trove of history in detail within the documents from around the time of the First World War, and some relating to a period of time even before that.

Respectfully, Emma looked more closely, carefully turning pages to find detailed records of class names and numbers, with the teacher's names included and the relevant dates. There were even records of sports days with the details of prize winners in the sack race, the egg and spoon race and other events. It was really fascinating. There were also some photographs.

The photographs looked really old with the children in long Victorian style dresses or breaches and wearing bonnets or flat caps. As she looked closer, Emma could recognise some of the family names as being the same names of people she knew who still lived in the village: The Smith family from Back Lane who used to run the blacksmiths, the Sheridan's and the Robinson's.

Well, what a discovery, she thought.

Emma couldn't wait to tell Rory and indeed to inform the village community. She thought that she could make up a display to show in the pub. She wondered if any people in the village would be interested. Emma really hoped that they would. What a wonderful discovery, she felt really excited!

Later, Emma continued her enquiries by looking in old church and parish records and discovered that some of the boys in the photographs went on to be soldiers and were killed in the First World War. One family had lost two brothers in France only to lose their third son who survived the fighting only to die as a result of contracting influenza in 1919. He was actually buried in the village church yard.

As she toured around the graveyard, she saw the vicar approaching her and was able to tell him about her findings. He seemed genuinely pleased and encouraged.

'I think that's really significant,' he remarked. 'It would be good to see you in church, Emma.'

'Oh sorry, vicar, not my bag I'm afraid,' replied Emma, hoping that he wouldn't be offended.

'Oh, that's a shame,' he replied, looking disappointed. 'I suppose that's why you chose not to get married in church?'

'Yes, I suppose it was, simply opting for a church wedding purely for the photos is not enough, don't you think?'

Oh well at least the girl has integrity, he thought.

She left thinking her find had deepened her sense of connection with the village. She had been able to sit where previously people had written school records of the life and times of village residents long ago this somehow felt to be a privilege but at the same time almost an intrusion. Emma felt that it almost brought the school back to life. She felt an immediate responsibility to hang some of the pictures in the house. What a find and what a lovely surprise it had been.

***

Gary's team were nearing completion and attention was turning to the outside space. The area that they had designated for car parking just needed a new layer of tarmac and the garden could be developed later as a secondary consideration. At this stage, they decided not to bid to rent the extra piece of land adjoining the property, feeling confident that it would be likely to come on the market again at some point when they might have a greater need for it, and hopefully be in a better position to afford it.

Hedges and fencing were in a relatively good condition so they agreed to leave that part of the gardening for Rory to manage. Gary still felt that some of the old playground would be suitable to simply cover with new slabs to act as a patio and BBQ area. To do that would about exhaust their budget, so they agreed to make that Gary's last task.

Shortly afterwards, the month's notice had been served on their rental property in Millfield and Emma and Rory were able to move into their new house with the aid of a hired van and the assistance of a few friends. They completed a last walk round the property with Gary and, when the inspection was complete, they were very pleased with the final results. The old school had been transformed into a family home comprising of: an attractive hall area; two offices or storage rooms to one side; three bedrooms – two completed one with en-suite; a family bathroom; and a large open plan living dining area with a wood burner. Aside from this room was a large well-equipped family kitchen with ample utility space, a separate toilet and a second wood burner. The second burner was a basic design with no glass front and access from the top via a lid with a substantial wooden handle. This would utilise any rougher pieces of wood and larger logs and provide an ample supply of hot water, as well as heating that part of the house.

Other features could follow in the years to come but they had achieved their aim of creating a family home in a place where they wanted to settle and bring up a family. It had stretched them financially, and absorbed much of their time and energy in recent months, but they were so pleased and proud of the results.

Other village residents called in to see the results of their labours and to wish them well. People seemed to be pleased that the school had returned to a vibrant place and been put to good use as a family home. Glasses were raised to toast their arrival and success. The local pub landlord was kind enough to provide a few sandwiches and a buffet on the bar for their first night in residence, which was very kind after a busy day moving. The atmosphere in the pub felt welcoming and helped to generate a sense of belonging. They both felt contented that they had arrived at a place that they wanted to be!

Chapter Twenty-Two

Early days in the new house were great, with Emma taking charge of adding some tasteful final touches to make a home. As she had predicted, Rory was happy just sitting and staring at the wood burner, eagerly awaiting the autumn season to begin. He set about planning the garden – some extra lawn would need to be laid and a few extra trees and shrubs would be useful, he decided. Emma wanted pots and outdoor lights and some stylish outdoor furniture.

Rory thought that he would need a shed and to start to build up a collection of tools. After his father had died, his mother had wanted to remain in the family home, but she had accepted now that it was too big. Many of his father's things, including garden tools, remained unused and were available to bring to the new house.

After the revelation about his father, neither Emma nor Rory felt that they could really forgive his mother and had all but broken off contact. Discovering that Rory had been adopted, and therefore the man he had known as his father and grown up with was not actually his father at all, had been a painful experience. His mother had maintained the pretence until his father had died and the truth eventually came out.

Maybe now, however, is the time to start to rebuild bridges, he thought.

Collecting some tools could be a means to re-establish contact, at least on a practical level. Rory didn't feel so disconnected that he didn't want to take advantage of any of his adopted father's possessions. Making use of some garden tools seemed like a fairly neutral beginning and was a practical solution to providing the means to create a garden at the old school house.

Emma went shopping for household items, leaving Rory to research into sheds. A fairly substantial one seemed justified as they had no garage. Rory had not previously needed to own tools and garden equipment, having lived alone in rented accommodation for many years, but he was now looking forward to establishing a base, including collecting some of the necessary equipment. A good drill, he felt, was a suitable starting point, so he determined to research the availability of local suppliers and to visit some car boot sales in the hope of picking up some of the basics – a hammer, some screwdrivers and spanners and whatever else he might find.

Bracken seemed happy in his new home as he rushed around investigating all the new areas to sniff and search. They had brought his old bed with them so he had some sense of familiarity. Together they were starting to explore the local area and some of the walks available from the house. Rory did miss his walks along the canal bank but soon found new and interesting footpaths to follow, including an old droving route. The path ran between two farms, over a hill and around the mere, ending up at the pub before heading off towards Newport. At least the new routes meant less occasions of returning with a soaking wet dog stinking of canal!

In those early days, village life seemed all that they had dreamed of. They made some good friends, enjoyed their visits to the pub, which was conveniently just around the corner from their house. One couple they met regularly in the pub were teachers at the local junior school at Gnosall and had moved into the area from Stoke the previous year.

Damien and Michaela originally came from Essex but had moved to Stoke to experience northern city life in an area where they felt confident that they could secure their first posts. Trying to find jobs in Essex was much harder they had found, with multiple applicants chasing each job. They quite liked the friendly and welcoming nature of the people that they had met in Stoke but, on balance, preferred the relative quiet of village life.

Damien had offered to help Rory in the garden, which he appreciated as he really didn't have much of a clue about horticulture. Damien had learnt about gardening as a child working with his father and had cultivated a large garden in their new home. He grew a good selection of his own produce and was keen to help Rory get his vegetable patch established. He told him about crop rotation, composting and planting whilst Rory listened with interest and was eager to learn.

***

People were friendly and there were a regular selection of events running in the village, from quiz nights and an annual bonfire party to some clubs based in people's houses. The village church didn't have the influence it used to have on the local community and the old parish rooms had long been sold off. The vicar was a nice man but was very busy and seldom present in the village as he had four other local churches to service. He had often said that he wondered what would happen over the next ten years or so as the elders of the respective villages died off and church attendance would continue to fall. Young people, he felt, too often only looked to the church these days for a picturesque wedding venue, as Emma herself had suggested. Baptisms and even funerals were not regular events anymore. He found that people often opted to go straight to the local crematorium and miss out the church service all together when their loved ones passed away.

Talking to an older resident, Emma discovered that, before the local school closed, there were two general stores in the village and a fish and chip shop. One general store doubled as the post office and the newsagent and the other concentrated more on selling fresh farm vegetables. Before that, there was a blacksmith in the village, and a chimney sweep, and bread and milk deliveries were common place.

'The village is not what it was, then?' Emma asked the elderly gentleman.

'No of course not, my dear. Things move on but not always for the better. There isn't the same sense of community that there used to be and too many people come into the village these days with no understanding of rural life and just want to use it as a dormitory town, and I don't like that.'

'Oh, that's a shame, but we really want to live here,' she replied, keen to establish her sense of belonging.

'Oh, so I've heard, my dear. I wasn't referring to you. We need more young people like you who want to raise a family here. That could even make a case for reinstating a school.'

'Yes, I hope so, but not in my house!' she added.

***

Rory chose his shed and placed an order for a twelve by ten-foot version with a simple sloping roof. A section of the old playground acted as a sufficient base to build it on and, once the delivery men had lifted it off the lorry and erected it in situ, it looked just right. Rory set about fitting some shelving using the drill that he'd selected from the available options. Then he could start to arrange some of the tools that he had collected from his mother's.

She had readily agreed to him taking whatever tools he wanted and was actually out when he called so any initial embarrassment was avoided. Rory was pleased to have made the first move towards a possible reconciliation. He hoped that was realistic. He was equally pleased with his acquisitions. The shed was starting to look well organised already.

Emma had selected the rugs that she wanted to spread over the wooden block floors. Then she could begin thinking about curtain poles. More use of Rory's drill followed in fitting a selection of wooden and black forged metal poles from which to hang the curtains. A local craft shop had been able to supply a suitable wooden name plate to fit by the front door, announcing the transition to the old school house. Some of the children's cloakroom pegs were able to be reused in the hall and one old black board found a role as a family note book in the kitchen. Being able to write notes and shopping lists in chalk was useful and felt appropriate, they agreed.

By now, Emma was only working one day per week in Birmingham with her old firm and was enjoying the challenge of establishing her own business. Rory was also busy trying to keep a track on progress with the house whilst concentrating hard at work. He was keen to keep a close eye on developments with Karl Pritchard.

Rory managed to fit in a visit to Karl at last. As he approached HMP Garth, he thought that it had been a while since his last visit to this particular prison. He went through the usual security and search procedure and was escorted to the visits room, where he waited for Karl to arrive. It wasn't long before he appeared through one of the gates and an officer pointed out where Rory was sitting. Karl walked across and looked better than Rory was expecting.

'Hi Karl, sit down. You OK?' he asked.

'Not too bad, Rory. It's good to see you.' Karl replied. 'Sorry I've had my head up my arse, but that's how I've been feeling. I've settled down a bit now that the end of my sentence is approaching.'

'Well, that's good then. Yes, I didn't pursue coming to visit because you would have refused to see me.'

'Is that what they told you? The bastards!'

'Well, I'm here now. So, Karl, have you learned anything this time?'

'Oh yes, Rory. Don't get caught – this is just too much hassle!'

'And how about don't do it in the first place, Karl? Sentences will only get longer.'

'Yeah, you're right but it's hard when you've got no money and people are on your back; you don't think straight and you do daft things,' said Karl, miserably trying to justify his own actions.

'Yes, well you *DO* need to think Karl, to think of the victims and think of the consequences for them as well as for you!' said Rory trying to break through and make a point to Karl, hopefully in terms that he could understand.

'Yes, easy to say now. Maybe you can help me get a job, Rory. That would be useful.'

'Would you keep it?' Rory asked.

'That depends if it was any good,' Karl replied instinctively.

'Well, we need to try, Karl. Have you done any education or work-related training since you have been here?'

'Yes, actually I have. I've done some maths and some reading and I'm on the waiting list for a forklift truck driver's course.'

'Can you drive then?'

'Or do you mean have I passed my test?'

Rory sighed.

'Yes, I can drive and no, I haven't passed my test, but I don't think you need that for forklifts.'

'OK, well let's hang on to that. The other major thought is accommodation, Karl. How about some kind of supportive community project?'

Rory went on to describe what that might be like and its advantages to Karl who at least didn't dismiss it out of hand. Rory felt that he had got somewhere in planting the seeds of an idea when the alarm bell sounded warning of an incident somewhere in the prison and officers appeared quickly to take all the prisoners from the visits room back to their cells. They said a quick goodbye, Rory said that he'd talk to Karl's mum and Karl was gone.

It had been worthwhile, Rory considered as he drove back home. He stopped at a service station for a cup of tea and phoned Karl's mum to tell her how the visit had gone. She sounded reassured.

***

Several months later, Emma was feeling more tired than usual and a bit emotional and she couldn't work out why. She told Rory that she felt 'funny' and he tried to be sympathetic and advised her to go to the doctors if it didn't get any better.

It wasn't long before the cause of her change in behaviour became apparent when she discovered that she was pregnant! Rory was delighted, Emma felt a little apprehensive but he tried to reassure her that it would all be fine.

'That's easy for you to say, Rory. You are not the one carrying the baby!' she remarked with feeling.

'No, but women have been bearing children since time immemorial, Emma!' he replied in a matter-of-fact way that only a man would consider appropriate. Predictably, she instantly burst into tears, which was unusual for Emma. Rory had to concede that he had said entirely the wrong thing. He was reminded of a comment that an uncle had said to him once along the lines that women needed a lot of love when they were pregnant and he thought his old uncle was probably right.

Rory had to learn quickly to adapt to their change of circumstances and to be more attentive to his wife as the pregnancy progressed. Emma didn't experience many of the problems associated with pregnancy but did feel quite anxious about the prospect of giving birth. Many of her friends had been through it, some with no concerns and others with quite horrific tales of the less palatable aspects of the process.

They started to collect nursery items and baby equipment as time went on, much of which was donated freely from other families in the village, which was kind. Emma was finding the effort of maintaining the house and her business was getting harder, even without having the added work of looking after a child.

She was really getting quite anxious about the prospect of being a parent and how she might cope. She knew that her mother would be no real source of help or support, and that she would need to look to friends to fill the gap. People in the village almost regarded the impending birth as a communal event and talked about the child as if it belonged to all of them. One day, Emma called Rory at work and asked him to come home early. When he dutifully arrived, she was terribly upset.

'What on earth's the matter, dear?' he enquired as he walked through the door wondering why Emma suddenly felt so wobbly.

'Oh Rory,' she cried. 'I don't know whether I can do all this!'

He just managed to avoid telling her that it was a bit late now and tried to be supportive.

'Come on Em, you'll be fine,' he said without feeling wholly convinced.

'Do you really think so, Rory? I've never done this before,' she said nervously.

'No, but you have overcome all sorts of challenges that were new to you at the time, Emma,' he said honestly.

She continued to cry and he sensed that there was something else bothering her. She had been a bit quiet lately he thought.

'It's also the village, Rory. It's not the house, I love that,' she spluttered as she tried to explain.

'Everyone has been so kind, but I'm not used to people assuming such closeness so easily. Some of the neighbours act as if it's going to be their baby and that they have a master plan to look after it between them. It's almost like they don't want me to be involved!'

Rory wasn't sure how to respond.

'I was so looking forward to village life, but it's not really what I expected. Half the village are never here and don't take part in anything and the other half seem to know everything about you and what you are going to do next before you do!' she announced with feeling as the tears continued to flow down her cheeks.

Oh dear, thought Rory as he tried to acknowledge her dented expectations.

'Oh, Emma. It's probably just being pregnant as much as anything; your hormones are all over the place,' he said almost immediately wishing that he hadn't as she slammed the door and stormed off towards the bedroom.

What do I do now? he thought. Do I go and try and console her? Or do I leave her alone for a while? He decided that the latter was probably the best option so went to put the kettle on in anticipation of her return to the main living room shortly. He waited. After a while, he thought that he had better go to see if she was alright and walked over to the bedroom and popped his head in cautiously.

'Are you alright? Would a cup of tea help?' he offered kindly.

'Yes please. I'm sorry, Rory. I'm not usually like this.'

He just sat beside her and held her close, thinking that was probably the best thing to do before he made the tea.

She joined him by the fire and sat down blowing her nose hard and wiping away the tears. 'I wish my mum was more supportive and was really there for me.'

'Maybe we need to make more effort, Em? We had rather cut her off, don't you think, before I contacted her about the garden tools?'

'Yes, but you know why.'

'Obviously, but maybe it's time to move on, to build bridges?'

'You are probably right,' she acknowledged.

'Did I hear you OK? Did you say I was right?' he replied as they both laughed and the tension eased.

Later, after making them both some dinner, Rory asked her, 'Can you say what it is exactly about the village that you think is missing, Em?'

'Um, I've been trying to put my finger on it. Something one of the older residents alluded too; village life has changed and maybe I'd just bought into the image too much.'

'OK, image as against reality?'

'Exactly,' she replied. 'He said that there used to be two shops, including a post office, and that the church had a village hall and other facilities. Maybe that's why some of the villagers seem to put so much hope on this baby, as if it's going to revive the village's prospects!'

'How do you mean?'

'Well, the loss of the school was because there weren't enough children born in the village,' she replied.

'Oh, I don't know, Em. I can't see the council reopening village schools now; there aren't many left, they are too expensive to maintain and, anyway, they can't have the building back, can they?'

'No, of course not. I said that, too. Thanks, Rory. Thanks for trying to understand. I'm so glad I've got you,' she said lovingly.

'It will be alright, Em. Yes, of course village life has changed over time, but we can make it what we want it to be, can't we? We can maintain goodwill with other members of the community, but we can also make it clear that we value our independence and keep some of them at arm's length, don't you think?' he said, trying to be positive.

'Yes, yes of course we can, Rory. You're right...'

'Again, that's twice today, you realise!' responded Rory as they laughed and hugged and held each other tight.

Chapter Twenty-Three

Afan had deteriorated rapidly in custody and eventually was transferred to the Hatherton Centre medium secure psychiatric hospital in Stafford. There he was able to be stabilised and be properly assessed. Once the correct combination of medication was established and supervision ensured that he was taking it properly, Afran started to improve. He became more communicative and less insecure and confrontational.

The diagnosis was not straightforward, with clarity obscured by years of drug and alcohol abuse, however the medical team seemed confident that Afan was suffering from a combination of depression and anxiety coupled with some difficult personality traits. He struggled to trust people, he had attachment difficulties, he was fundamentally insecure and could be violent. Intervention would not be easy. The prognosis for successful treatment and potential independence was deemed to be poor.

Efforts were made to find Afan suitable accommodation for eventual discharge. No conventional hostels would take him. He would need some form of specialised provision. After some research, a possible placement was identified in a voluntary project in rural North Wales. It was run by a charitable trust and offered long-term placements for people with mental health problems and difficult personality traits. Staffing levels varied between more comprehensive supervision on induction to semi-independence for those who responded well to the regime and had made sufficient progress. Some limited work was included to service their own needs, and gardening and animal husbandry were also found to be therapeutic.

This seemed a suitable placement for Afan and an application was made on his behalf while staff tried to explain their reasoning to him to reassure him and gain his consent. Afan seemed to understand the staff's concerns and it did feel like they were doing their best to find him the right place. He knew that he couldn't survive on his own and would need permanent help and support.

***

Things were going well for Rhys. He was enjoying his education and hoping to do well enough in his A-levels to go to university. That would be his route out, his escape, his sanctuary. However, events seemed to conspire against him and things did not turn out to be so straightforward when a local rugby match turned sour.

Rhys played fly half for his local team and was a good game manager and a reliable kicker at amateur level. They were due to play their local rivals and these matches had a history of tension and confrontation. Both sides were keen to dominate and to gain local bragging rights. The previous year, the police had got involved in a post-match disturbance. No action was taken but both teams had been warned about their conduct.

This year, efforts were made to build bridges, to play down the historical context and just enjoy the game. This approach seemed to be successful until late in the second half when a dangerous and recklessly high tackle led to a nasty neck injury with one of the players from Rhys's team being stretchered off. Emotions were running high as the referee called time with the score drawn at fifteen all.

The supporters were frustrated both by the lack of a clear winner and by the injury to one of the players. They grumbled as they left the pitch to dissect the match over a few beers in their respective club bars. By late evening, both sides were well-oiled and should have gone home but unfortunately a small group from Rhys's team decided to settle unfinished business. They had heard from the hospital that their player was in serious trouble and would need urgent surgery on his neck with some inherent risk of paralysis. This instantly inflamed passions and they set out to wreak havoc and revenge on the opposition. They armed themselves with sticks left over from bonfire night to fashion improvised clubs and walked across the fields the relatively short distance to the opposition club.

By the time they arrived, the members were in full voice with *Bread of Heaven* ringing from the bar. When Rhys heard a whisper of their intentions, he immediately smelt trouble and set off to try to stop them. As he arrived he could hear mayhem in the club house and sirens in the distance. Despite his best efforts to calm things down, by the time the police arrived in force the situation was well out of hand.

The police were prepared and came ready to deal with a likely public order disturbance. Shields, batons and pepper spray were all generously deployed before mass arrests rounded up the bloodied protagonists. Some saw it coming and managed to leave the scene in time, but the hardcore were caught and detained. With Rhys still desperately trying to hold people apart, he was arrested too and statements taken the following day were too confused and contradictory to support his assertion that he was not actively involved in the fracas but was trying to calm things down.

Given his family's reputation, being a Howell on this occasion didn't help him as the police readily assumed that not only would he naturally be involved but that he was probably one of the leaders. Given the history and the warning from the previous year, the outcome was inevitable; twelve local men were eventually charged and remanded in custody pending trial for various public order offences. The Crown was determined to make a point and all twelve men were subsequently sentenced to six months in custody.

A short sentence in practice can sometimes have little impact other than inconvenience and embarrassment, but for some it led to loss of employment, debt or was the last straw in a failing relationship. For Rhys it proved to be critical. Later, the disruption to his studies contributed to him failing to secure the grades he needed in his exams and shattering his hopes of a university place and an escape from what he saw as a predestined life of chaos and self-destruction. Being labelled a 'criminal' didn't particularly bother him, nor the relatively brief experience of custody, but the disruption to his plans was a bitter blow and one he would not forget or forgive easily.

He found sitting in his cell to be a salutary experience. He reflected back on his life: his relationships with his inadequate mother, his absent father and his dysfunctional brothers. He also remembered the day on the causeway when David Jackson had lost his life. He thought about Elis and Rhian, he thought about David and he thought about Mr Evans. Rhys knew that Mr Evans was not responsible for David's death and, sitting in his cell at that moment, albeit only serving six months, made him think how it might feel to be serving nine years when you too were innocent.

***

Elis was coming to the end of his sentence and was looking forward to release, not particularly about going home but about revenge – that was what was on his mind. He knew from some of the other lads inside that one of the men who had attacked him was already dead from a drugs overdose. It reminded him of one of his father's famous sayings: sell the stuff but never use it. So that left two others still around to satisfy his blood lust. Revenge would be sweet, he promised himself. That was what kept him going and was on his mind on the day of his release.

Elis glazed over as prison staff went through his licence conditions and told him that he must report to probation on arrival back in Porthmadog and that non-compliance would result in breach and the likelihood of a return to custody. He wasn't listening. He walked out of the prison gates alone to an unwelcoming world. His clothes didn't fit and he felt uncomfortable. The first thing he did was to go to McDonald's and buy some decent food, as he saw it, then he found a barbers, had a proper haircut and managed to avoid the temptation to end up in the pub. He bought some cheap trousers and a shirt and used his travel warrant to head for home.

Elis walked through the town that he had grown up in, with its dull and dismal familiarity. Nothing much seemed to have changed while he had been away. He didn't see anyone who was immediately recognisable as he made his way to the probation office. He called in briefly, as instructed, if only to avoid being breached and the risk of being returned to prison.

He carried on through the town towards home, where he had no expectations of a welcome and sadly his expectations proved to be realistic. He arrived in mid-afternoon to find his mother drunk and asleep, sprawled out on the settee. There was no food in the cupboards and little left in the fridge. The kitchen was a mess, with leftover food and unwashed pots scattered across all the work surfaces. The bin needed to be emptied and was overflowing with used pizza boxes and takeaway cartons. The floor was sticky with mud, grease and grime built up over a long time spreading everywhere. The dog's filthy bed was still in place but there was no dog to be seen.

No one else was around as Elis made his way through the hall between piles of old newspapers and magazines and dirty clothes stacked up against the walls. *What a shit hole*, he thought, as he smiled thinking that even prison was cleaner than this!

He wondered whether his father was living there at the moment or not. He didn't know. He couldn't detect any signs either way. Elis assumed that Glyn would be doing his usual act of popping in and out of his mother's life when it suited him. He hadn't heard anything from his father for a long time. He was disappointed that Glyn hadn't gone to visit him in prison, but he had to acknowledge that he was not surprised.

There was a cough and a splutter from the living room as Bron awoke, not expecting to hear someone else in the house. 'Is that you, Glyn?' she called out.

'No mother, it's me,' answered Elis.

Bron moved off the settee, lit up a cigarette, poured herself another gin and staggered out of the room towards the kitchen where she found Elis trying desperately to find a single cup clean enough to risk drinking from.

'Oh hello, Elis,' she said tamely. 'I wasn't expecting to see you, dear.'

'I did write, Mother, to tell you that I was going to be released today,' he responded indignantly as she made a notional attempt to kiss him. Her breath stank and he drew back away from her in disgust. Time away had highlighted just how dismal his mother's circumstances had become. Elis did feel some sympathy for her but really, he was just disappointed that she had failed to even remember that he was coming home that day.

'The post is so unreliable here, dear,' she offered as an unconvincing excuse.

'Mother, this place is filthy. What's been going on? Where's Dad and where's Mutt?' he asked.

'Oh, it's just a little untidy, dear,' Bron replied with the practised ease of self-deception.

'I'm going to have a tidy round tomorrow, then it will be fine. Your dad's not around at the moment – away on urgent business, you understand, and I think he has the dog with him.'

'Mother, I'm not a child anymore. Dad has no business and he was never here anyway. I'm going out to get some food!' shouted Elis as he slammed the door behind him and tried to negotiate his way out of the front garden through piles of rubbish and debris.

'Bring me back some ciggies, love,' his mother shouted behind him as he left, taking no notice.

Oh well, he thought to himself. *Back home, such as it is*.

Chapter Twenty-Four

Staff continued to monitor Karl Pritchard closely in HMP Garth and noticed that once again he was not keen to receive visitors and his general attitude had deteriorated. His behaviour fluctuated but staff could tell that he was not well. Resources were stretched and there was little prospect of any psychiatric assessment or treatment, even if he had been referred. Rory did feel somewhat uncomfortable about his limited capacity to support him. Funding and authority for prison visits were getting even tougher to secure. He couldn't justify a further visit if Karl was not going to see him or to engage in any meaningful discussion.

Rory had given some more thought, however, to Karl's release arrangements. He recognised that Karl would need specialist support and had identified a voluntary project in North Wales that he felt might be suitable. If approved, it would necessitate transferring the case to the Welsh authorities. Laura, his team manager, had briefed him about a possible case transfer of a high-risk offender, as it happened, from North Wales to Staffordshire.

'Elis Howell looks like a handful, Rory, but he has a job prospect in our area apparently and the local police really want him out of town. He has been referred to MAPPA and the Public Protection Unit are due to visit their counterparts in North Wales to discuss the case and possible transfer. Didn't you say that you may have found a suitable place for Karl Pritchard in that area? I wonder whether there might be some scope for an exchange of interests here.'

***

Elis could see no prospects for him in Porthmadog and started to think of alternatives. He had met a bloke inside who came from Staffordshire and said that his dad ran a scrap metal business and that he might be able to offer Elis a job. He had several caravans on site and employed a variety of people, with accommodation included. Elis had his number and decided to give him a ring.

'Hi Brummy boy – it's Taffy here. I'm out. What about that job you promised me then?'

'What?'

'Come on, you remember me – your pad mate from inside.'

'Oh yeah, Taffy, right?'

'Yes mate.'

'OK, I'll have to ask my dad, Taffy, but it's not the best time at the moment.' And he rang off.

Oh well, I tried, thought Elis.

He rang again the next day.

'Brummy, it's Taffy again, any news?'

'Oh yeah, my dad said that's OK. Things are quiet at the moment but he could do with one more lad. Cash in hand like, no guarantees and, of course, you'll have to pay for your bunk in the caravan. You won't earn much but it'll pay your beer money.'

'OK then, thanks. When can I start?'

'You can start whenever you like, mate.'

Elis told his probation officer on his next appointment that he had a firm offer of permanent employment with guaranteed accommodation in Staffordshire and wanted to move quickly to take up the offer. He said that this could give him an opportunity to make a fresh start with a reputable employer and initially his probation officer agreed and congratulated him on his initiative.

She could check out the details later, she thought.

***

MAPPA: Multi Agency Public Protection Arrangements lay out a protocol in law for agencies to cooperate, share information to improve risk assessment and manage high-risk offenders in the community. The Public Protection Unit staff in Staffordshire had talked to their colleagues in Wales and the case had been referred, with all the necessary background information, to a panel that was due to meet the following week to discuss the suitability of the transfer. Previous experience and enquiries had long suggested that informal arrangements for case transfer between areas or temporary management was not safe or satisfactory. Responsibility for case management had to be active, clear and agreed.

When the panel met, all the necessary information had been supplied, liaison undertaken and outline plans made and checked. Taking on responsibility for Elis Howell could well prove problematic, but that was in the nature of things. It was also apparent that he had overstated the nature of the 'job offer' and that it was definitely neither permanent nor secure. Behind the scenes, the leverage of potentially being able to place Karl Pritchard in the project in Wales was attractive to Staffordshire so a degree of willingness to cooperate and good will was already established.

In principal, the transfer was agreed. If the placement failed, Elis could always be transferred back but there were good reasons for wanting him out of Wales, at least in the short term. It came as no surprise to Rory that the case was going to be allocated to him. At least it kept the door open for a move for Karl Pritchard and that he felt was worth it. If Karl did transfer, Rory felt that he would be much more likely to succeed and stay in North Wales than Elis was likely to stay in Staffordshire.

***

Elis was pleased with the initial reaction from probation and started to collect some things to take with him. Not much was retrievable from the house, with his few possessions either having been used by someone else or having become covered in mould and mildew.

He needed some money so decided to visit someone who owed him from before he was sent down. He lived someway out in the mountains, Elis remembered, so he would need a car. He knew where one was kept that nobody officially owned and the keys were left in it in a lock up garage, and he knew where the garage key was hidden. He hadn't got a driving licence or insurance, but that wasn't going to stop him.

Elis collected the car and drove off in the direction of his contact. He wasn't surprised to find that the tank was nearly empty, but he had time to call into a local petrol station. He managed to put together ten pounds to buy enough petrol for his journey. Just as he was leaving, he noticed two men in a car three aisles down from him who looked familiar. He looked again and yes, he did recognise them – the two characters who had assaulted him that day with baseball bats. Without further thought, he quickly got into the car and set off to follow them. He was unprepared but maybe this was his chance to get even, he thought.

The two men drove in the direction Elis was intending to take out of Porthmadog, so he followed them towards Snowdon and onto some winding mountain roads. Elis followed at what he considered to be a sufficient distance not to be too obvious. *They couldn't have noticed me*, he thought. The two men seemed to be chatting away and not really concentrating on the road. It was dark and conditions were not good. Elis continued to follow them at a discreet distance as they wound around the steep roads.

Should I, could I? he wondered. *If the road gives me an opportunity to nudge them off it and force them to crash, should I take it?* It wasn't the way he had envisaged seeking his revenge, but it could be a good option with a fair chance of avoiding suspicion or detection.

The more he thought about it, the more he liked the idea as he drove closer and closer to the back of their car.

Then came the chance as the car in front faltered around a very sharp bend.

The driver wasn't concentrating and he misjudged the bend entirely, allowing Elis to creep up close enough to bump into his bumper and side panel. It felt like a substantial crunch as Elis smiled with satisfaction as the car in front carrying his two assailants slid and bounced over the kerb. It continued down the slippery steep bank gaining momentum and running out of control. The car gained speed, bumped and crashed its way down the hillside until he saw the car burst into flames and disappear into the depth of the valley below.

Elis had stopped, he couldn't believe it – this was better than he had expected. *Surely they must be dead*, he thought. All he needed to do now was to burn out his car. *I'd better get away from the area quickly*, he decided. I'd better take the car to somewhere where it looks like joy riders have pinched it and burnt it out, leaving no trace of me behind. Then I can walk away and no one will ever know. *What about my money?* he remembered. That would have to wait. This was more important. He could roll some poor unfortunate anyway, if he was desperate.

When the police became involved, they were neither surprised nor particularly concerned about the deaths of the two men in the car. They were trouble. No witnesses had come forward and it was not unusual for cars to veer off the local roads at night in poor visibility. Nothing was suspected. There was nothing left in the wreckage that suggested anything other an accident. The subsequent police investigation was therefore minimal.

No suspicion was attached to Elis and, as he predicted, the police assumed that the burnt-out car had no connection with the road incident and was the work of joy riders. Elis had achieved his aim. *You win some, you lose some*, he thought. That's what they had told him in prison.

Chapter Twenty-Five

Circumstances for both Karl and the Howell brothers were about to change rapidly.

Arrangements had been completed independently for the referral and transfer of both Afan and Karl. They arrived at the project in North Wales at about the same time. Karl still had no formal diagnosis of mental illness or impairment, but it was obvious to the staff filtering referrals that he was a suitable candidate. They had managed to negotiate an effective level of mental health support from the local hospital trust and were confident that Karl could be properly assessed in due course.

Both men understandably felt some anxiety about their placement but also an overwhelming sense of relief, both to be out of prison and to be somewhere where people seemed to understand and accept them. The project was realistically likely to be the best possible option for both of them and they responded well initially to the opportunity presented to them.

***

When Elis arrived at Brummy's yard, he took a look around. It looked rough. It was rough. He had to check in with the local probation team, which he did remember to do. Brummy looked different in his working clothes and the two laughed and joked about the contrast with being inside.

Brummy's dad was obviously a man of few words and simply showed him his bunk in one of the caravans and told Brummy to show him the ropes. He then drove off in a cloud of smoke in his old pick up with a mangy dog at his side.

Rhys was gutted; he was three grades off acceptance for a university place and too low to secure a place through clearing. He would have to retake his exams and apply again the following year. That would cost him money and delay his aspirations. He was frustrated, but he also felt uneasy.

Time reflecting in custody laid heavily on his mind. He felt guilty about Mr Evans, but he knew that, if he was to take the actions that he was thinking about, it would have significant consequences. He felt unsure how things might work out, but he knew in his heart that it was the right thing to do, even if it would cause ructions.

Events were moving fast for the Welsh boys. Significant developments were in play for all three Howell brothers; the boys from a deprived and disrupted background. The boys no one gave a chance. The boys who were destined to come to nothing.

***

Elis had gone to Shrewsbury with the scrap yard crew for a large contract breaking up some old industrial machinery. The trip was to take several days and he had forgotten about his probation appointment and that he had already missed one appointment previously. At lunchtime, he received an unexpected message from Rhys. The text simply said, 'I need to see you'. It was followed by a second message: 'Where can we meet in Shrewsbury?'

Elis was both pleased and intrigued. *What was so important and so urgent?* he thought.

He suggested meeting in a pub in the town, one which Rhys would easily find, and suggested that they meet at six o'clock the following day.

When the brothers met they shook hands, it had been a while since they had seen each other. They caught up on news and talked about old times until Elis asked 'So what's on your mind, Rhys? What was so important to want to meet all of a sudden?'

'Elis, I feel uncomfortable. You know what it's like sitting in a prison cell knowing that you didn't do it. It eats away at you. The injustice burns inside you.'

'Yes, so what? Shit happens,' Elis replied in a matter-of-fact manner.

'Well, sitting in my cell this time I thought of the situation at the rugby club and how no one would believe that I was trying to be a peace maker and was not responsible for what happened. Injustice, Elis, I couldn't get it off my mind and then I thought of Mr Evans, the PE teacher. He was a decent bloke, Elis. He didn't deserve all that flack over David Jackson. I think it's time to come clean, don't you?'

'No way! The guy must have nearly finished his sentence by now, why should we speak out? No, leave it alone, Rhys.'

'But the guy wasn't responsible, you know that. It's not right, Elis,' replied Rhys passionately.

'The little shit deserved what he got anyway. Arrogant English bastard. He turns up in our patch and expects to jump straight into our rugby team, demands to be captain, makes eyes at my girlfriend. What did he expect? Me to just take it? Well, he didn't know me then did he?'

'So were you right then to push him over the cliff? I saw you, Elis.'

'Yes. I went back along the causeway once the group had broken up and made a run for it. You and Afan followed me, if you remember. David had let go of the rope and had slipped on the wet grass. He was lying on the edge when I got to him. He put his arm out for me to grab it and pull him back, but I nudged him forward instead,' Elis replied.

'So you did push him over, why Elis?' Rhys asked.

'Because I hated the little shit. It was worth it to see the look of absolute horror on his face as he slid over the edge,' admitted Elis callously.

'You don't deny or regret it then?'

'No. No way.'

'I'm going to tell them, Elis. I have to. It's the right thing to do. For once in my life, in our miserable lives, this would make a positive difference to somebody else.'

'Like who?' Elis responded with both disbelief and fear.

'Well, obviously Mr Evans, for a start, but also David's parents and really everyone else who was there, Elis. They all deserve to know. Don't you think that's right?'

'No. Get away – you're fucking mad!' Elis replied in total disbelief at what he was hearing, not thinking for a moment that Rhys would actually say anything to the police. Another of their father's golden rules... don't grass... *Surely he couldn't break it?*

They sat and stared at each other trying to work out what the other was really thinking. How well do we actually know each other, Rhys pondered. After a long pause they changed the subject, finished their drinks and left the pub. They walked away without turning back heading in different directions. Rhys had been careful and anxious to ensure that the tape recorder worked. At the first opportunity he played back his recording and it was perfectly clear.

***

When Rhys went to the police in Porthmadog the following day, he was not expected and they were very surprised to see him. He asked for Sergeant Rashid or DCI Machin and was told that Inspector Rashid had transferred to the Met and Superintendent Machin was busy. He persisted and said he was sure that she would see him; it was about David Jackson.

After a while, Karen Machin appeared with a new inspector and led him to an interview room. He wondered whether she had guessed what he was about to tell her. He remembered thinking that she did not seem convinced that Deri Evans was entirely culpable at the time of the trial.

They sat down and looked at each other across the table, thinking back to the day of the incident, thinking of the causeway and of the consequences.

'I've come to tell you the truth about David Jackson,' said Rhys calmly.

'It wasn't an accident. Elis killed him.' As he handed over the tape, he added, 'This is all the evidence that you need. He pushed him over the edge.'

The superintendant listened intently.

'Are you sure, Rhys?' she asked gently.

'Yes, ma'am.'

'You know what this means?'

'Yes.'

'Why Rhys and why now?' she asked, not unreasonably.

He explained about his feelings, his time in the cell and his concerns for justice – his wish to right old wrongs. He knew what would happen to Elis and that the family would disown him. He didn't care. He wanted a new start and he wanted the system to help him.

Rhys wasn't sentimental, his attitudes were hardened by bitter experience. In his view, both his brothers Elis and Afan had the capacity for self-destruction anyway and therefore his intervention was not going to make the critical difference. He had agonised with himself and was satisfied in his own mind that his reasoning was based on more than just making him feel more comfortable about his decision. It was simply the right thing to do. In some ways, it felt like an attempt to redress all of the bad things that he had done himself. It felt like making a new start.

The two officers listened to the tape in private. It was unequivocal. They took a detailed statement from Rhys and negotiations got underway immediately.

'He'll have to move out of the area, Inspector. We can't have him here. I'll talk to Staffordshire. They won't be getting Elis now, but they might take Rhys.'

The situation was explained to Staffordshire police and probation and arrangements were made promptly to transfer him to police cells in Stoke for his own protection while temporary accommodation could be arranged. A hostel placement whilst on licence wasn't appropriate, as he would be recognised and exposed too easily. He needed to effectively disappear for a while.

Laura was called to an urgent meeting with the police about the Welsh boys and opted to take Rory with her.

'Sit down both of you and thanks for coming,' said Inspector Shaun Elder. Laura had worked with Shaun before and felt that she could trust him.

'You know the situation by now. Rhys Howell has provided concrete evidence that his brother Elis was responsible for David Jackson's death back in 2003. Elis has already missed two probation appointments so, with your cooperation, we can pick him up and get him locked away safely back in custody. The Welsh police are going to charge him with murder so don't anticipate him staying around to complete his licence. Afan will need to be interviewed, but he seems stable in the project in Wales, and Rhys will need to move out of their area. A transfer to Staffordshire has been agreed above our level and we have to make it work. Rhys just wants to retake his A-levels and get to university. He's a brave lad; he knows what's at stake here.'

'Yes, OK, Shaun. We can do this,' said Laura confidently. 'Rory will be the case manager for continuity. He knows the background. Rhys will no doubt complete his licence and we can exercise some discretion in his favour in the circumstances. We just need to keep it quiet. If he gets to university, the heat will be off and hopefully he can get on with his life.'

'Great, thanks to both of you,' replied Shaun. 'You do realise that nothing can be discussed about this case outside this room. There must be absolute confidentiality between the three of us. No mention to colleagues and certainly nothing beyond, that includes at home.'

They all nodded. Shaun was pleased to secure their cooperation and knew that he could trust them, given his confidence in what had become a well-established working relationship.

'What about Deri Evans?' asked Rory.

'Good question,' replied the Inspector. 'He will be informed of the new developments in prison and I'm sure will want to seek appeal on that basis. The logic for him is immediate release.'

'How do you pick up your life after that, poor man?' posed Rory.

'Quite,' replied Laura.

Chapter Twenty-Six

Elis returned from Shrewsbury expecting to get paid well for his efforts. He wasn't impressed to have been charged such an excessive rent for his miserable bunk in a damp old caravan and was remonstrating with Brummy's dad when the police arrived to pick him up.

'What! What now? What do you bastards want?' he asked as two officers climbed out of the first car. They obviously weren't expecting a warm welcome. A scuffle ensued before handcuffs were applied and Elis was led away and placed between two burly officers in the back of the second car.

'What about my money?' he shouted to the scrap dealer.

'It doesn't look like you're going to need it now, son!' was the curt reply.

Elis was interviewed under caution and couldn't believe how much the police claimed to know about what he'd said to Rhys.

'What's my little brother been telling you? The little creep!' he cried out.

'We will interview other members of the original group, Elis, and we will make a strong case against you,' the arresting officer replied. The interview continued with Elis getting more and more irate as it became increasingly obvious that the police had him wrapped up nicely. It wasn't long before his actions gave the officers the opportunity to add assaulting a police constable to the charge sheet as he hastened his own demise.

When the police arrived to interview Afan, he was very reluctant to say anything. He said that he vaguely remembered moving back along the causeway following Elis but claimed to have no recollection of what happened next. The officers sensed that he was rattled and was probably protecting Elis but knew that they weren't dependent on his evidence so didn't push it.

As the officers left, Afan was livid. *Who had split on them? Who had grassed them up?* Afan asked himself and knew that it could only be one person. 'Dad's golden rules,' he ranted. 'Number three... don't grass!'

Staff had been disappointed to see such a rapid decline in Afan's mood and in his behaviour following the visit from the police. They were increasingly concerned about him. They hadn't seen him act like this before. Since his arrival at the project, Afan had generally been calm and even quite placid. Now he was clearly angry and agitated.

***

Rhian had held onto her story for all those years and, in some ways, it was a welcome relief to be able to tell the officers what she knew.

'I didn't see him push David, but I somehow knew,' she said. 'I could read the look on Elis's face when he came back to the group. I knew David was missing. I had danced with David at a house party while Elis was away one weekend playing rugby and I knew that it would get back to him. Someone told him that we'd been smooching and he was mad. He didn't like David anyway but after the party that was it as far as Elis was concerned. He saw him as a rival and, from then on, his card was marked.'

'What exactly do you mean by that, Rhian? Do you mean that you felt Elis was planning to harm David?' asked one of the officers, trying to gain a greater understanding of what was happening preceding David's death.

'Oh no, I don't think that he planned it. He was just set on being against David and on putting him down whenever he had the chance,' Rhian replied insightfully.

'Do you think, in wanting to put him down, that he would go as far as killing him, miss?'

'I don't know about that, but I do know that Ellis had a temper and could react violently against anyone that he thought was against him.'

The officers paused for a moment and tried to assess the significance of what they had just heard. It didn't seem to them that Elis's actions were exactly premeditated, but he did appear to have the capacity to be vindictive.

Rhian sighed. 'You do know that I got pregnant at the time and had an abortion, don't you?' she asked.

'Yes,' replied the officer.

'Well, the child wasn't his, you know. It wasn't Elis's baby – it was David's. Things got out of hand at the party and I was pregnant sometime before I started sleeping with Elis, but he was so conceited that he automatically assumed that it was his. My father was against him from the start and, when I had to tell him that I was pregnant, then that damned Elis in his eyes even further.

'I made up the allegations about Mr Evans too, they were all completely false. I've always regretted it, but it felt it was too late to say anything. I only did it to try to protect Elis, to take the investigation away from him and to add weight to the case against Mr Evans. It was spiteful, I know, but I was only young. I'm settled now, with a proper family, respectable. I don't want any upset.'

The officers thanked her for her honesty and left. Whether charges would result against Rhian would not be their decision, but she clearly had lied during an important investigation and contributed to the downfall of an innocent man.

***

Momentum was established and events continued to move quickly from that point. Elis was charged with murder and remanded in custody. Breach of licence and assaulting a police constable would be taken into consideration in his eventual sentence and, significantly, they would help to make a case for a remand in custody – not that, given his record, he had any realistic chance of bail. If he was to be found guilty of murder, a life sentence was inevitable and, given his history, a long tariff also seemed likely.

Mr Evans was released on appeal and all charges against him were withdrawn. He had more than paid the price for any responsibility he had for the context of the events that day and was left a broken man. His wife had left him during his time in prison. The media attention and hostility from the local community had been too much to bear and she had moved abroad to start a new life.

He could not return to teaching, not that he wanted to, nor did he feel able to return to North Wales. He had few savings, little equity from the divorce settlement that had been orchestrated by his wife, and his pension pot would be minimal. He may be able to improve his pension later, given the circumstances, but it was clear that he would need to do some sort of work to sustain himself in the meantime.

His health, both physical and mental, had suffered during his time in custody and he felt lonely and isolated. He tried hard not to be bitter, but it was difficult to avoid such feelings. Only one friend from his teaching days had stayed loyal, stayed in touch and had supported him throughout his prison sentence. As another member of the PE staff, he had proved to be a true friend and was his anchor now.

In court, proceedings were swift. Legal advice to Elis was that there was no room for manoeuvre. Electing to plead guilty meant that there was no need for a trial, no involvement of a jury, just the conclusion and remarks of the sentencing judge. Elis wasn't listening, but the judgement was damning in the light of both his actions and the length of time before his eventual admission. The judge also noted the attitude of the offender; Elis showed no sign of either regret or remorse, indeed he seemed to celebrate the actions that he had taken. The Judge concluded that he was a very dangerous man and that the public had a right to expect to be protected from him in the future.

Within two days of Elis being sentenced, Afan was found hanging from the window frame in his room. The sense of betrayal by Rhys and the consequences for Elis were too much for him to deal with and he had taken his own life. Glyn tried to take the moral high ground and, acting as the father of all three boys, declared his fury towards Rhys and vowed to avenge Elis. He blamed Rhys for Afan's death and for Elis's imprisonment. It was no more than Rhys had anticipated but he was very sad to hear about Afan.

For Bronwen, however, this was devastating news; for a mother to lose a child is heart-breaking enough, but to lose a child to suicide was almost unbearable. *How had things turned out so wrong?* she thought. *How might it have been different?*

Elis, she knew, always had the potential to ruin his own life and those of others. She wasn't surprised about how things turned out for him but was nevertheless disappointed. Afan, however, was a sensitive child. He needed to be cared for and he had been sent to a place that was meant to do just that and they failed him. They let him die and she couldn't find it in her heart to forgive them for that. His loss hurt far more than the almost certain knowledge that another son would end his days in prison.

What of Rhys? she wondered. She never felt very close to him. He always seemed somewhat different, as though he didn't really belong. He would do well, she supposed, but was he happy? She didn't know, she hardly ever heard from him now. He was ashamed of her, she supposed.

Rhys proceeded to complete his A-level studies and to retake his exams. He managed to improve his grades significantly and he was delighted to secure a place at Manchester University to read politics. He found that, despite this poor start in education, his break from it and his subsequent life experience helped him to better understand the political landscape that he was studying. He discovered that he could do well at university.

Rhys preferred to avoid the conventional student culture of parties – heavy drinking and late nights – preferring instead to concentrate on his studies. He appreciated the opportunity to look beyond the boundaries of his previous miserably limited horizons, which was both liberating and exciting. Despite his posturing, Rhys never heard anything more from Glyn and wasn't surprised.

Rhys graduated with a first-class honours degree and went on to complete a masters studying in America and a doctorate based back in the UK at Liverpool University. He developed a particular interest in social justice issues, social exclusion, equality of opportunity and criminology.

Rhys settled in Liverpool and remained a radical and a non-conformist and, after a short period working as an academic and university tutor, he went on to work for a think tank and research institute, attempting to influence and advise the government on criminal justice issues. Throughout his career, he wrote and published various influential papers on crime, justice and social policy.

He never returned to the area of North Wales where we grew up. Nor did he seek any further contact with any of his family, and he didn't miss them or regret his decision to distance himself from them. He never married nor brought children into the world, not wanting to taint them with any sense of what he regarded as his poor genetic inheritance, nor did he feel best equipped to be a parent.

He continued to believe that he had made the right decision in exposing Elis, despite the consequences. He considered that he had helped to enhance understanding of deprivation, having had some influence on government policy, and therefore he had been able to bring some good to the world. Rhys derived some satisfaction that he'd done his best to make a success of his life in spite of his humble beginnings.

Rhys attempted to avoid the impact of his experience leaving him cynical or angry, although such feelings did rise to the surface periodically. He tried to adopt a realistic and balanced view of the world and to recognise many of the positive aspects of human endeavour.

Elis reappeared on Rory's caseload as a life sentence prisoner with a tariff of fifteen years, the minimum term that he would serve before any consideration for release by the parole board. Elis surprisingly seemed to get over any sense of resentment against his brother. In a perverse way, he almost admired him for his honesty, a characteristic that he didn't share. He had no regrets, however; he never pretended that he was anything other than pleased that he had killed David.

Oddly, Elis saved his wrath for David himself, who he blamed for interfering in his life, and for Rhian, who he discovered had 'slept with the enemy'. Elis could be cold, calculating, vengeful, and focused almost entirely on his own interests. He was not motivated by prospects of rehabilitation, so he resigned himself to a lifetime in custody and adapted to build walls around him. He formed his own gang, ran protection rackets and learnt how to adapt to drug dealing in prison. He kept the authorities at arm's length and was careful not to readily fall foul of too many prison rules.

There followed long years of moving between different prisons of countless assessments and re-assessments by seemingly endless different staff, all largely reaching the same conclusion. The overriding picture that emerged was of a man satisfied with himself, rigid, resistant to change and stoically uncooperative. Elis consistently either paid lip service to any rehabilitative course or was positively disruptive, engineering his own deselection from the group.

After fifteen years, he had served his tariff and had the right to consideration for release by the parole board, if he was deemed to present little or no risk to the public. At this point, Elis did recognise some potential incentive in cooperating with the authorities and did make some attempt at engaging with the parole process.

Despite this, however, he was not surprised when he was informed that his first parole application had been unsuccessful. The board had recommended that he undergo a full psychiatric assessment before any further consideration for release in another two years' time. Elis did agree to meet with the doctor and to answer his questions. The report concluded that he had strong psychopathic traits and was unlikely to change. He didn't disagree, in fact, he quite liked the status of being referred to as 'a psychopath' and accepted his fate. He knew that such a diagnosis made his chances of ever being released much harder.

He reinforced his position in the prison hierarchy with his gang around him. He shunned what little contact he had with outside. Knowing his likely fate, he became more belligerent and more determined to make his life as easy as possible and to make things as difficult as he could for the authorities. He would not be broken. He was almost content. David could not break into his realm again.

Chapter Twenty-Seven

Rory had thought about putting his proposal to Emma and felt that he was ready to present his argument. He rehearsed it in his mind as he drove home that night through the winter cold, looking forward to sitting by his log fire.

'Hi Em, I'm home!' he shouted as Bracken bounded over to greet him.

'Hello, love. Had a good day?' she enquired.

'Yes actually, and I have something I want to talk to you about,' responded Rory enthusiastically.

'That sounds ominous!' replied Emma. 'If you are thinking of launching an expedition to the African jungle, best count me out,' she said, glancing down at her growing bump.

'No, it's not that…'

'Thank goodness!'

'Actually, let's sit down with a cup of tea by the fire.'

By this time, Emma really was intrigued.

'Go on then, tell me!' she said eagerly as they sat down.

'Well, you know that my team have to lose half a post, and you know that the management committee for the pub want to appoint a part-time project manager. Well, I wondered if I ought to apply for it…'

'Oh, that,' she said nonchalantly. 'I wondered when you'd work that out. Of course you should apply – it's made for you. Just do it!'

'Really, so you agree?'

'Yes, it won't pay as well, presumably, but we can accommodate that. It will be good experience for you, you'd enjoy it and be good at it and they want somebody local who is committed to the idea of a community pub.'

'Marvellous! Love you, Emma.'

'Right, you'd better take Bracken for his walk and I'll put the dinner on. Jacket potato and beef stew alright?' called Emma as the boys rushed out through the door.

He looks so excited, bless him, thought Emma. *He'll call in at the pub now and tell them, then try to tell me that he hasn't!*

Rory set off at a pace straight for the pub to tell them the good news. He burst in with Bracken pulling hard at the lead to meet the landlord's dog, who was guarding the bar whilst sitting next to Sam the chair of the management committee.

'Emma has agreed that I should apply for the pub project manager's post. What do you think?'

'Oh, she has already told us and we have you pencilled in. You're just the right man for the job. When do you want to start?' said the chairman.

'Well, I haven't even completed an application yet and there may be others who are interested. When are you thinking of holding interviews?'

'Oh, never mind with all that. Pull him a pint… you're appointed. You start now, or as soon as you can move to part-time at probation,' replied the chairman, wishing to keep things simple and with no enthusiasm for protracted process, as he gestured to the landlord.

'OK,' said Rory, feeling a little overawed and excited. 'What about the salary?'

'Oh yes, don't worry. We'll pay you as well, with a start date sometime after Christmas for an initial period of three months. Now drink your pint – cheers!'

Rory drank up and took the congratulations before leaving with Bracken for a quick march through the lanes in the dark, thinking that was the easiest approach to job selection that he had ever experienced and envied the simplicity and flexibility of a small project like the pub! *What if probation didn't release him?* he thought. *He'd be working time and a half then!*

When the boys burst back into the house, Emma had prepared the dinner and it was nearly ready.

'Emma, Emma, guess what?'

'You haven't been to the pub, have you?'

'No, well, yes actually… and I've got the job!' he replied.

'What took you so long?' she responded, knowing that she had spoken to the committee chair earlier in the week.

Rory spluttered, 'But aren't you pleased?'

'Yes dear, well done. I'm very pleased, and so is bump, and I'm sure Bracken is proud of you too!'

***

The following day Rory spoke to Laura. 'Can I have a brief word about the loss of the half post please?'

'Oh, don't worry, Rory; your job is safe. We'll probably find a way to lose it through natural wastage.'

'That doesn't sound very nice! It's just that I have decided that I want to apply.'

'Oh no, Rory. I can't lose half of you!' she cried.

Rory explained about the pub and the brewery and that he had accepted an offer of taking up a part-time post as project manager/coordinator.

'Oh, well done. That must have been quite competitive?'

'Yes, it was an extensive selection process,' he replied, smiling.

'OK well, if you are serious, I'll mention it to HR. I'm not sure how far they will have got with it. They might want to advertise it as a new part-time opportunity, and you'd have to apply with anyone else.'

'OK, or couldn't I just go part-time, independent of the reduction in posts?'

'You could, Rory, but I already have two shared posts. That's four people to manage rather than two. I really don't fancy splitting another post.'

'OK, well, I'll leave it with you then,' he replied hoping that it would work out.

Oh dear, this could get complicated, he thought, but he was prepared to run both jobs in the short term as he considered that they could use the extra money with the baby coming along.

Rory started to think about how the pub might widen its use as a community hub. It was big enough to include a small shop, or at least an exchange facility for those growing fruit and vegetables to bring their produce and barter. Similarly, they could run a book exchange – take a book to read and return it for a pound a go maybe? The same service could be run hiring CDs or DVDs. A post office would take more work and research, no doubt. Maybe they could even run a bed and breakfast facility? With no one living in the pub, they could alternatively rent the accommodation to generate some income. He started to order his thoughts to be able to write a discussion paper to put to the committee with some ideas and some options.

There was also scope for useful community information, he considered. People could offer their services as, for example, gardeners or babysitters or offer items free 'to a good home', like unwanted furniture. They would also need to recruit an army of volunteers, if all the services that he envisaged were to run successfully.

When the committee next met, Rory was introduced as their appointee and people were both pleased and excited by the prospect. He had emailed his options paper to them all in advance for their consideration prior to the meeting.

'Welcome everybody,' announced the chair once they were all comfortably sat in the bar area.

'Right, let's start by considering some of Rory's ideas. I must say that this is an excellent start, thank you!'

'Yes, I agree,' added Edward the solicitor as the others nodded. 'I'd be happy to explore the issues around opening a post office,' he said.

'OK, accepted. Note that!' the chair nodded to the secretary.

Another member with bar experience offered to look at rotas and start to establish a list of suitable volunteer bar staff, and to consider some basic training. Two of the local mums, Becky and Claire, had already offered to start things going in the pub kitchen, selling sandwiches initially and then to try some simple hot dishes and perhaps fish and chips early evenings on Fridays.

Setting up the shop/lending idea wasn't urgent and they decided that it could wait until later, perhaps as more of a spring/summer facility, they thought. After all, there were plenty of other tasks to attend to if they were to open by early summer.

The easiest way to establish the idea was probably not to call it a shop anyway, but an exchange. People could bring their surplus home grown produce – fruit, vegetables, jam, cakes and so on – and swap items or leave them for others to take away for a donation to community funds. That idea had scope to grow and, with open access and an honesty box, it wouldn't actually need anyone to run it, at least not regularly.

No one else had thought of renting the flat above the pub and they thought that was a great idea and a good means of generating some much-needed revenue.

As regards the post office, later Edward was able to report that he had made initial enquiries and that the process wasn't going to be quick or easy, but that it was possible. That may well have to be a future objective they concluded, but it would be a prize worth fighting for. A post office was not only a very useful local facility, but a symbol of success and independence for a village community.

Through the autumn the people of the village pulled together. They were able to undertake the necessary work to be able to bring the pub up to the required standard. Whilst that did involve some technical work for the various village tradesmen, it mostly required willing hands and enthusiastic voluntarism. The electrician, the plumber and the local builder between them managed to fit in most jobs around their normal schedule. Rory provided some coordination and continuity and the volunteers shifted materials, painted and cleaned as the project progressed.

On a typical day when the pub renovation project was in full swing Emma suddenly found herself feeling uncharacteristically overwhelmed when her washing machine stopped working and she walked in to find the kitchen floor was flooded. She just felt tearful and silly at the same time and wasn't sure what to do when the village plumber who had been working on the pub walked past her window on his way to collect some tools from his van.

He saw that she was crying and, although they had only met once before, came to her aid without hesitation. He simply walked in, smiled and offered to sort it out for her. Within a few minutes, he had identified the problem as a hose that hadn't been connected up properly and had become unattached, hence flooding the kitchen as the washing machine emptied its dirty water. He replaced and reconnected it, found a mop and cleaned up the floor before making them both some coffee. She felt that he was so kind and understanding and that it was another indication of the existence of community and the spirit of human kindness if you could just find it.

When he returned to the pub to carry on, he found the others having a break and discussing progress. They had concluded that the pub wasn't in too bad a condition overall but, now that the brewery had removed all of their belongings and most of their equipment, it did look a little tatty. They had to admit that the living quarters certainly did need some significant level of renovation and, with some effort, funds would have to be found to be able to replace and update both the bathroom and the kitchen.

The bar area mainly needed decorating and, with guidance from the builder able volunteers, they were able to construct some fitted bench seating along the back walls of the bar, which looked very homely once cushions and some upholstery were applied.

As autumn progressed, the villagers turned their attention towards Christmas. With the pub still being too much of a building site to be used for any form of gathering, several people opened their homes to guests for social events and parties, which were well-received.

The village was coming together as a community. The pub had provided a focus for their attention and energy to work together to bring a new energy to the notion of village life in a way that worked for them and was flexible enough to accommodate the demands of modern life. Old romantic notions needed to be redefined but they found that the spirit of mutual help and support was still as relevant and beneficial as it ever was.

For Emma and Rory, their first Christmas in their new home was special. Rory dug up a Norwegian spruce from the garden for use as a Christmas tree in the living room, which looked lovely with the glow of the fire adding to the effect of the lights and the decorations. After some difficult encounters, they did manage to re-establish at least a cordial relationship with the woman they now referred to as Emma's mum. Rory had accepted her too in her true role as his adopted mum. He had also accepted that he could never experience a family relationship with his real parents and didn't feel inclined to want to seek any further information.

Mum joined them for Christmas Day to enjoy a traditional family celebration. Christmas dinner was prepared between them without fuss or argument, with the turkey and 'pigs in blankets' supplied by the local butcher.

Rory could see that Mum was relieved about their renewed contact. Further explanations, and any expectations of apologies for all that had gone on before, were carefully avoided and the focus of their attention was to look forward rather than back. Rory hoped that Emma and her mum would be able to help each other and enjoy the baby together and it seemed that, for the first time, such an aspiration could become a possibility.

With a final burst of energy in the New Year, work continued in line with the target of completing the necessary renovation work and making the pub presentable. Costs were kept to a minimum and the element of community participation helped to consolidate precisely the spirit they were trying to establish.

One of the tradesmen knew a contractor who was going to be working in the area on HS2 and was looking for accommodation for six months. The timing worked out well when the landlord was offered an alternative pub with the same brewery not too far away in Newport. The village wished the couple well and the contractor moved into the flat in January, providing a much-needed boost to their funds.

The pub reopened under new management, keeping its old name, earlier than originally envisaged in May 2017, despite some unexpected delays in completing the project. Virtually the whole village came out to witness the event and the pub nearly sold out of beer! The kitchen was on full production, making bacon and sausage sandwiches and serving two different homemade soups with freshly baked bread rolls. Everyone enjoyed it and lots of people joined in to help. Initially, filling the rotas wasn't a problem but, after a few months, it was becoming apparent that a more permanent solution was going to be needed.

It was decided that there was sufficient funds to offer some remuneration to the two mums running the kitchen and to employ a cleaner two hours per day. The pub opened initially on Wednesday to Sunday, with scope to open more days if it generated sufficient trade.

John, the member of the committee who had previous experience of a community pub, had done some further research and discovered a successful working model run in Hawes North Yorkshire. They wanted to engage the services of a local brewery, not only to supply good local ales but to help with the management of the pub. Other members agreed that this was a good idea and Rory was tasked with approaching Titanic brewery, whose help had already been sought to provide some free advice on setting up the pub and had supplied some of their excellent beers.

Steerage, as a relatively low alcohol beer, proved to be popular as well as Anchor and Iceberg as the mainstays. They looked forward to introducing a wider range of beers as trade picked up; they anticipated that some of the stronger darker ales, such as Captain Smith and Plum Porter, would also be popular. The pub also served some of the more mainstream brands of both beer and lager to try to appeal to all tastes. John tried to be helpful but other members of the committee were growing tired of his constant remarks about how good things were where he lived before to the point where people did start to wonder why he had moved or indeed wished that he would go back if it really was that good!

Rory was keen to make this work and wasted no time in speaking to Dave Bott, one of the brewery directors. Dave and his brother, Keith, had established themselves as shrewd business men and avid supporters of the growing micro-brewing industry. Dave was helpful in discussing some ideas and readily recognised the issues that Rory was describing. Previous experience with other similar pub projects in the area provided some guidance to follow, and some indications about what had worked elsewhere.

After some thought and negotiation, the committee and the brewery decided on a hybrid model, with partial management contracted out to the brewery, but with a substantial role being maintained for Rory, or whoever may follow him as the local community representative. Dave suggested that the day to day running of the pub (i.e. staffing and ordering stock) was best done by the brewery. By this time Becky and Claire were ready to handover responsibility for the kitchens to Dave to organise, but they were still prepared to assist on a voluntary basis.

Edward had helped in placing the project on a sound official basis, with proper business records, accounts and legal agreements. A constitution was drawn up for the management committee, with an annual general meeting for all shareholders to hear of progress and exercise their voting rights.

The committee also agreed to extend Rory's contract for another three months.

They were pleased with the contribution he had been able to make, but all of them accepted that there may come a time, when the new arrangements were fully established, that his post might become unnecessary or at least reduce in scope and hours. They also recognised the reality that the project had to work hard and produce some revenue in any event if the post was to remain affordable. This had been made clear to Rory from the outset and he accepted the limitations and the risks.

In April, the brewery had appointed a friendly young couple to be the new landlord and lady, conveniently about the time that the HS2 contractor was ready to leave the flat. They agreed terms and arrangements to take over. They were relatively new to the pub trade, having both recently left the forces. They anticipated moving into the flat in June. In the meantime, one of the villagers was able to offer them temporary accommodation in their house.

Once they started work in May they quickly settled in and soon became accepted as the custodians of the pub. They were at first amused but did start to feel a little irritated by villagers' constant references to being 'shareholders' and therefore entitled in their view to special treatment. This could take the form of expectation of generous measures or preference when asking to book a table or even as blatant as demanding discount off their bill.

Rory had to politely inform people that being a shareholder brought more responsibilities than privileges, a message that was not always well-received! John particularly tended to take offence at Rory's interventions and revert to harping on about his past experience.

Rory had moved to working part-time at probation in April, much to his relief, and in the end without too much process involved. The change had been ring-fenced to the local teams and, in the event, he was the only officer expressing an interest to move to part-time so his application was accepted without delay.

By the time the new couple were settled into the pub, things were set to be running relatively smoothly as the year progressed. Rory therefore needed to start to consider what he might do to secure a second part-time income. He had enjoyed the experience and didn't want to simply return to full-time employment with probation but to extend this arrangement or something similar. He also wanted to be involved in due course to assist Emma with the care of the baby.

Emma's pregnancy was progressing well and she remained in good health. All the indicators and tests suggested that the baby was also doing well.

Rory then had time to build his chicken shed. The garden tools that he had acquired proved their worth. In fact, having just bundled them up and brought them home from mum's, as Rory selected them and used each of them, they did actually invoke some happy childhood memories. As he held them in his hands in turn, he could imagine Dad using them or he could remember them doing garden jobs together.

Perhaps I should make more effort to see the positive aspects of my childhood, he thought, after all he was nurtured and there was genuine warmth in the family.

The disappointment and sadness had only come with the revelation about his adoption and all the feelings that were aroused at the time. At least having these tools gave him some sense of history, if not exactly belonging, and maybe that was something valuable he considered. Especially, he thought, after they had all enjoyed a family Christmas together.

As the chicken shed took shape Rory felt more and more comfortable working at home. He had a growing sense of satisfaction that, in some small way, this experience had helped him to begin to adjust and anticipate the next stage in their lives.

By the end of the day, the shed was complete and ready for occupation, including the installation of a gate and some fencing to keep the chickens safe and secure. He had bought ten hens from a local farm that morning. He took advice on which breeds were the most healthy and reliable and which produced the most eggs. Emma was keen to use the eggs as much as she could but also to give some to the shop in the pub as that became established.

Rory constructed his log store as a sturdy construction on the back of the house, making use of easy access from the kitchen. Logs could then be readily brought into the house to service both burners. The kitchen wood burner design proved to be a success with its simple construction and top loaded access. As they had hoped, this made it suitable to place larger logs or awkwardly shaped pieces together with those that proved difficult to split. The fire in the living area by contrast needed relatively uniform sized logs and, with the glass panel in the door, provided a ready view of the fire, which added to its appeal. Rory had discovered just how much timber two log burners could get through! Fortunately, one of the local farmers supplied large quantities of seasoned fire wood at a reasonable price. Sometimes Rory was able to help him in exchange for more wood.

***

Emma and Rory set off for a short walk with Bracken. She passed by the copper beech trees around the water from where the village derived its name. Emma was beginning to feel that the baby would be due soon. She thought of their wedding; the ceremony, the vows, the speeches and the chance to catch up with friends. She thought of her overriding feelings of love and how much she had enjoyed the day.

Whilst Rory threw sticks for Bracken, she thought about their honeymoon in the Cape Verde islands: how the locals would collect fish fresh from the harbour in wheelbarrows and take it home, how tourists were strongly advised not to risk swimming in the sea with its strong currents and the prevailing high winds. Then she thought about their weekend in Wales, the walk in the hills and the friendly family at the bed and breakfast; a warm vision of how contented she hoped her family would be. Then Emma's thoughts turned to her memories of the school tragedy where she remembered that a boy had died. That he was found at the bottom of a cliff he must have fallen from. She remembered the media frenzy and the cruel treatment of the school teacher in charge.

'Are you OK, Em? You look deep in thought,' Rory asked as he joined her with Bracken and walked along slowly by her side.

'Yes, love, it won't be long now. I was just thinking about all our happy times and then I remembered that boy who died in the mountains and how badly that poor teacher was treated.'

'Yes, he went to prison, you know?' Rory remembered.

'Yes, I thought so. I wonder what happened to him after that,' Emma said.

'He was exonerated in the end and one of the other boys was found to have pushed the poor lad over the cliff.'

'Yes, love, I seem to remember that was what happened. How would you recover from an experience like that if you were the teacher?' she posed.

'I don't think you would,' Rory replied.

***

In time, Deri Evans did manage to find some meaning in his life. On release from prison, initially he accepted an offer of accommodation with his friend who had supported him throughout his ordeal. By then his friend had changed schools and was living in Shropshire, which provided a safety net for Deri away from North Wales with all its bad memories.

He realised that his employment prospects were going to be limited. Even though he was no longer regarded as a criminal, or could be considered to be a risk to children, he had nevertheless been out of mainstream employment for some time. He needed to work and wanted to find a new direction but initially he needed to secure an income and get back into a working routine. On impulse, Deri took a job as a sales assistant in a sports shop. Whilst selling sports equipment he enjoyed the contact with ordinary people and began feeling like a person of some worth again.

He also enjoyed feeling quite anonymous.

Deri was surprised to find that he actually really liked the job. It gave him the opportunity to apply his knowledge about sport in general and wasn't too intense or demanding but most of all he relished and celebrated his freedom and the sheer relief from the daily grind of being in custody. He was enjoying life again.

After a trial period, to his surprise, the sports shop management offered him a permanent contract and promotion to head of one of the sections in the store. Initially, Deri almost felt amused by the offer but decided to accept it. He was enjoying the change and a return to having some responsibility.

Later, when the area manager visited and complemented him on his sales performance, he accepted a further offer of training and a move to manage a smaller store of his own. Deri had thought that he needed a change of direction and reflected that, without him searching, he seemed to have found it. He felt pleased to work in a different field but one where his previous knowledge and experience was still relevant.

Despite all the trauma, the disappointment, the sense of injustice and the frustration of all that he had been through, Deri managed to hang on to a feeling of belonging in a setting where he was still working with people and was part of a team. He began to feel that he had a future…

POSTSCRIPT

Summer 2017

On June 1st baby Poppy May Scott was born into this world a fit and healthy child.

Rhys continued to prosper while Elis remained in custody.

After Rhys's revelation about Elis's responsibility for David's death, the political storm continued to grow. In the corridors of power questions were being asked and arguments constructed to lobby for a change in the law. If Elis Howell was a psychopath, why had it taken so long before he had been properly assessed and diagnosed? Surely it couldn't be right, some argued, that he was left to kill before this was identified? Once it became apparent that he may have been involved in the death of the two drug dealers when their car 'accidentally' left a winding mountain road in poor weather conditions, the nature of the questioning became more intense.

The police could only conclude that it had been convenient to take the two dealers out of the system and therefore foul play couldn't be ruled out. Other rival dealers would have benefited and, of course, it was known that Elis had a strong grudge against the two men and therefore a motive.

Prompted by the media coverage, a witness did come forward claiming to have seen the car that was later found burnt out and thought not to be connected with the incident on the road. The sighting was at about the critical time and the car was said to be following the car driven by the two men who died. However, the witness was not confident that she could identify the driver.

It was known that Elis was one of several local offenders who had access to that particular car, but it could not be established beyond reasonable doubt that Elis had been the driver that night, nor that he or any other driver had contributed to the accident. The two damaged cars could conceivably have indicated that a collision had occurred but at the time one was broken into pieces at the bottom of a mountain and the other was a burnt out shell. By now both cars would have long been scrapped or recycled and there was no way of retrieving any evidence. No, the police had to conclude that the evidence wasn't strong enough to prove a case against Elis for anything related to this incident, from driving offences to murder.

Officers did visit Elis in prison to question him about any possible involvement in the incident, but he denied any knowledge of or involvement in the affair. He just smiled, leaving the officers to doubt his honesty but with no solid confirmation, only professional intuition based on his capability, motive and opportunity... if he had in fact been in that area at the time, he could well have been responsible.

The political debate continued. Why hadn't the police intervened earlier to stop the use of the car as they knew the drivers would no doubt not be properly qualified or insured? More pertinently, the question remained why should we wait to identify a psychopath until after they have been involved in murder? This was a much more difficult question raising some fundamental issues. Yes, Elis could have been identified as a possible high risk to the public far earlier than he was, but then how would the authorities respond? Would it be right to try to detain someone indefinitely because of concern about what they MIGHT do as opposed to what they actually HAD done? Psychopathy after all was not only linked to criminality, psychopathic traits are not uncommon in the more general population and, indeed, present in some very successful people – people who can be charming but ruthless.

We couldn't conceivably imprison them all!

A Look Forward

I hope you have enjoyed this latest story featuring Rory and Emma. I am already writing a further book in this series to continue their journey as they plan a change of direction and a new future. How far will their experience in Coppermere shape their aspirations and how will their plans unfold?